"The future co[...]
now," The Pr[...]
"Already the c[...]
But I can show [...] vision, so
you may see what is coming and
perhaps better prepare for it."

Reeling, Buffy glanced at Willow and Oz, then at Xander and Anya. They all seemed as stricken by the specter's words as she was. *Prediction*, Buffy told herself quickly. *It isn't fact yet. We don't know it's true.*

But it felt true. The words of The Prophet were heavy with finality. With doom.

Buffy swallowed, then looked at the oily silhouette again. "Show me."

"I must only touch you, and you may see."

"Do it," Buffy instructed her.

The Prophet's slick, shimmering form slithered forward. The tear in the fabric of the world extended toward her, fingers like tendrils reached for her.

"Buffy," Willow said cautiously, a tiny bit of fear tinging her voice. "Maybe this isn't such a good—"

The Prophet touched her.

Invaded her.

Buffy screamed.

Buffy the Vampire Slayer™

Available from ARCHWAY Paperbacks and Pocket Pulse

Available from POCKET BOOKS

THE LOST SLAYER

Part One

PROPHECIES

CHRISTOPHER GOLDEN

An original serial novel based on the hit TV series
created by Joss Whedon

POCKET PULSE
New York   London   Toronto   Sydney   Singapore

HISTORIAN'S NOTE:

This serial story takes place at the beginning
of *Buffy*'s fourth season.

An *Original* Publication of POCKET BOOKS

 POCKET PULSE, published by
Pocket Books, a division of Simon & Schuster, Inc.
1230 Avenue of the Americas, New York, NY 10020

ISBN: 0-7434-1185-4

First Pocket Pulse printing August 2001

10 9 8 7 6 5 4 3 2 1

POCKET PULSE and colophon are registered
trademarks of Simon & Schuster, Inc.

Printed in the U.S.A.

PROPHECIES

CHAPTER 1

All dressed up and no one to slay.

A chill wind blew off the Pacific Ocean. Buffy Summers zipped her navy blue sweatshirt up to her throat and shivered, just a little. All right, it was November, but still, Southern California in November was not usually quite so brisk. She was tempted to pull her hood up but there was something just a little too gangbanger about that look for Buffy's tastes.

As Buffy walked along the waterfront, she stuffed her hands into the pockets of her sweatshirt and grumbled softly to herself. Her gaze darted around the wharf and the canneries and the large shipping vessels out on the water. Sunnydale had its share of gorgeous California beaches, but this wasn't one. This was Docktown, the part of town the Chamber of

Commerce desperately tried to divert tourists from. In a way it was surprising these streets were still on the map.

Patrol had been completely uneventful thus far, and it was growing late. Midnight had come and gone and by all rights Buffy should have long since returned to her dorm. She had class at ten minutes to nine the next morning and she was determined not to oversleep. Now that college had started, she was turning over a new leaf. The Watchers Council held as conventional wisdom that a Slayer could not carry on a personal life and be effective in the war against the forces of darkness.

Come hell or high water, Buffy intended to prove them wrong. She would be the most efficient, most effective Slayer who ever lived. But she would also immerse herself in the college experience, both socially and academically. In high school, she'd failed to balance the two, had really made a mess of things a few times. But college was going to be different. Maybe she'd never be normal, but with the enhanced physical capacity that came with being the Slayer, she believed she could juggle it all.

If she managed to get to class in time in the morning.

What the hell am I doing all the way out here? she thought.

The answer came back quickly, and what a simple one it was: *the job.*

She was doing exactly what she was supposed to be doing. Buffy was the Slayer, the Chosen One, the one girl in all the world with the power to combat the forces of darkness.

Tonight, though, things had been quiet. Patrolling Sunnydale was a vital part of her work as the Slayer. But when patrol was slow, that was when a bit of doubt might creep in; doubt that she would actually be able to pull off the balancing act she was attempting with school, her mom, her friends, and slaying.

What she needed now were action, adrenaline, and a nice, juicy monster or two. See Buffy. See monster. See Buffy kick monster's ass. It was what she needed to keep her focus.

A scream rent the night air with the blunt brutality of a gunshot. A quick and violent instant that caused Buffy to flinch even as its echo died above the waves.

Despite the ominous quality of that scream and what it might mean, she could not hold back the ghost of a smile that flickered across her face. Heart pounding in her chest, Buffy sprinted along the wharf. Her legs pumped as she ran past the harbor-master's quarters on one side and a long, ugly concrete building that housed several shipping companies' offices. She waited for another scream but none came. At Dock Street she instinctively turned toward town and ran alongside a liquor store and half a dozen run-down multifamily homes mostly utilized as boardinghouses, renting rooms to fishermen and merchant sailors.

Halfway along the next short block she saw the

cracked and flickering neon sign that hung in front of The Fish Tank. Experience told her that was her destination. There was no activity out front so Buffy stopped short at the entrance to the stinking alley beside the bar, a place so sleazy calling it a dive would be an insult to dives everywhere.

No scuffle in the alley.

Buffy frowned. Her instincts could have been wrong. She looked around, alert for any sign that might lead her to the screamer. Patrol had taken her here before; The Fish Tank was just the kind of place that bottom-feeding vamps afraid to draw the attention of the Slayer liked to hunt, thinking it beneath Buffy's notice. It wasn't.

A muffled laugh came from farther along the alley, deeper in the shadows.

Something was going on there in the darkness, where things let out small giggles weighed down with sinister intent and gleeful perversity. It was amazing all the evil a laugh could contain.

Buffy ran the length of that darkened alley between buildings, then paused just at the corner of a building, her back to the brick wall. To her left there was a small paved area behind The Fish Tank lit by a single bulb above the back door. In its sickly yellow glow she could see an open Dumpster filled to overflowing with shattered beer bottles and the remains of what the place mockingly called food.

It was a narrow drive that ran behind a number of the small businesses on the block, and Buffy was amazed that somehow a garbage truck fit itself back there at least once a week.

It stank, sure. But more important, it was remote and dangerous, with the buildings on one side and a chain link fence on the other. It wasn't a place anyone would go by choice.

Yet somehow they'd gotten the woman back there—a woman all by herself.

Vampires.

Three of them crowded around the woman, who had screamed once and then had been unable to scream again. They were locked onto her as though they were entranced, one with his mouth on her throat, fangs piercing the soft flesh and a small rivulet of blood dribbling down to stain the collar of her Aerosmith T-shirt, and the other two at her arms, also suckling her blood but not quite as sloppily as the first. On their exposed skin Buffy could see markings, unfamiliar symbols she could only assume had some arcane meaning. The rest of their bodies was covered in leather.

The woman was maybe forty and had no business in the Aerosmith T-shirt and cutoff denim shorts she wore—unless she was a regular at The Fish Tank, where head-banging rock and hard drinking were the order of the day and a woman could be twenty-four and look forty, and still the guys would get all crazy around her.

What a life. Buffy didn't understand places like The Fish Tank or the people who went into them.

But she didn't have to understand to care. To act. To

take vengeance. Given that there were three vamps feeding off her, and the way she hung in their arms, completely limp, eyes without any spark, Buffy knew the woman was beyond her help.

Too late, Buffy thought bitterly.

From a sheath at the small of her back she withdrew a long stake with a smooth grip and a sharp, tapered end. She liked to feel its weight in her hand. With a single breath Buffy stepped out of the alley and into the dimly illuminated drive in front of the huge blue Dumpster.

The vampire whose fangs were buried in the woman's neck grunted and looked up at her. He had a black tattoo across his face, a bat with its wings spread, eyes peering out from inside each wing. A gnarled symbol shaped like a bonsai tree was carved into his face at the jawline. Bonsai's eyes narrowed.

At first Buffy thought it was just a trick of the jaundiced light, but then she realized it was no illusion. The vampire's eyes glowed a faint orange; a kind of energy seemed almost to radiate from him, to crackle around his entire body.

This wasn't like any other vampire she'd ever seen.

For a moment it threw her off. Then she chuckled and shook her head as she thought about how badly she had been itching for a fight. *Careful what you wish for,* she thought.

"I can't decide," the Slayer declared, her voice sharp and clear in the brisk night air. "Could be you're in a gang. Sunnydale Flying Rodents. Something like that,"

Buffy said, ticking off possibilities on the fingers of her left hand while still clutching the stake. "Could be you got lost on your way to some comic book convention. Or, possibly, you've just gone all freaky-geek over *The Matrix* and now have no life outside the film."

The vampires let the woman's lifeless form slump to the filthy pavement and she saw that the eyes of the others also sparked with that unnerving orange glow and exuded an aura of energy so different from other vampires she had fought. All three of them, it turned out, had bat tattoos across their faces, around their eyes. The overall effect was profoundly disturbing. They moved slowly toward Buffy, forming a half-circle around her, as if to prevent her from running away. Of course, she had no intention of running.

"Then there's always *D,*" she said idly. "All of the above."

All three of the vampires snarled at her, their fangs glistening in the dim light, eyes blazing. When they moved it was as one, a savage onslaught that would have made her think them barbarically stupid if not for the air of dark intelligence each of them had. Yet they were silent.

Buffy didn't like them silent. The ones who were cocky and boastful were easy kills. The silent ones were usually more dangerous.

With a single hiss they lunged for her. Buffy backed herself up against the metal Dumpster as if they had her cornered. Her lip curled with disgust from the stench and from the company.

She waded into them. The one on her right was inches ahead. She ducked past him, under his reach, then came up fast with her elbow and rammed it into the back of his head, cracking his skull between her bone and the Dumpster without ever looking at him.

Bonsai reached her more quickly than she had anticipated. Even as she turned to thrust her stake at him, he was on her. Powerful hands wrapped around her throat and he lifted her off her feet with a strength that surprised her. All vampires were strong, but this was something more. The creature thrust her against the Dumpster hard and her head clanged on the metal. Had she been a normal human, it likely would have been over for her then.

But she was not a normal human being. She was the Slayer.

Fireworks went off in her head and black circles appeared before her eyes. The beast choked her harder, and Buffy could not get even a single breath of air. Her eyelids fluttered for a moment and she felt a kind of terrible exhaustion, a dark fatigue, sweep over her. Though she beat at his face and chest with her hands, pulled at his fingers, she could not break his grip. She wondered if it was the vampire's somehow draining her of energy, or just the lack of air.

Not that it mattered which. The key was breaking Bonsai's grip on her throat. Over his shoulder she saw the other two, the one recovered now, just hanging back and waiting with hyena grins.

Those grins pissed her off.

From a primal place deep within her she summoned all the strength of the Slayer. With the Dumpster at her back, she hauled up her legs, planted her feet on his chest, and shoved him away. Her hands thrust up and her fingers clung to the top of the Dumpster. The other two ran at her and she swung her feet up and kicked them both away, then dropped to the pavement in a crouch.

While trying to break free, she had dropped her stake. Now she snatched it up as the trio ran at her again. Bonsai was in the lead. He came at her, barely defending himself, as though confident her escape was merely a fluke, that his power was superior. She thrust her stake into his chest and its tip punched through his heart. The vampire's eyes went comically wide, outlined by the black bat tattooed across his face, and then he exploded into cinder and ash with a muffled thud.

The Slayer was determined not to be surprised by them again, and not to let any of them get their hands on her. Whatever had supercharged them, whatever made their eyes burn with that dark orange glow, she thought it might also allow them to leech energy from a person the same way their fangs could leech blood.

The other two came at her fast. Buffy landed a high, spinning kick that knocked one away, but the other, whose body was the most heavily tattooed with arcane symbols, kicked the stake out of Buffy's hand. It went skittering along the pavement into the shadows. The vampire grabbed her by the hair and she felt some of it give way, her scalp beginning to bleed, as he hauled her backward to expose her throat. The face of the beast stared down at her, those orange, blazing eyes almost mesmerizing, and the vampire dipped his fangs toward her neck.

Buffy frowned deeply. *Can't let him weaken me any more.* She slammed her head up into his face, splintering his nose and causing him to stagger backward.

"What, are you kidding? You go up against me, you go for the kill, moron. That Nosferatu intimidation crap doesn't work on me."

Even as she spoke she moved in, fists flying. He tried to defend himself but the vampire had no hope. He had lost the upper hand and would not be allowed to get it back. Buffy spun and kicked him, bones in his chest cracking as he flew backward and slammed against the chain link fence that ran along the back of the narrow drive.

Buffy found the stake.

The two vampires rushed her again, and it occurred to her that these monsters were not only somehow enhanced, but also a savage but regimented breed. The tattoos showed organization, and organization among vampires was not only rare, it was a very bad sign.

Buffy snapped a side kick at the one on her right, then spun and shattered the other's jaw with another swift kick. He went down. She dropped down with him, stake in her hand, and then he was dust. The breeze off the ocean swept him away with the stink of rotting fish and stale beer.

On his knees, the survivor moaned.

Buffy kicked him over. He slammed into the Dumpster again. She grabbed him firmly by the throat and held the stake to his chest, just above his heart.

"The tattoos. What are they?" she demanded.

The vampire grinned, licked his own blood off his lips and red-stained teeth. The skin on his forehead was split, a wound in the image of the bat.

"I don't like that you guys are all marked the same. I don't like that you're so quiet. I don't like that someone's embellished the vampire formula here. I want answers. You can tell me what I want to know and die easy, or I'll stake you out buck naked on the roof of one of those concrete bunkers that pass for offices down the street and you'll burn inch by inch as the sun comes up. New and improved model or not, I have a feeling you'll still torch."

The vampire flinched, the thick ridges of its monstrous brow deepening, and a growl built low in his chest.

Buffy pressed the point of the stake hard enough so that it punctured the skin, put all the weight of her body on the injured vampire, and returned the same snarl the creature had been giving her. She kept an eye on his hands, just in case he tried to sap her strength as Bonsai had.

"This kind of marking, the way you guys move together. There are more than three of you. How many? Who's in charge? Where can I find them?"

"You won't need to find him," the thing growled,

his voice raspy and thick with an accent Buffy did not recognize. "Camazotz will find you. And his followers are legion."

"Where?" she demanded.

He laughed at her, a throaty, knowing, evil sound. Buffy stood up, kicked the vampire in the chest, then hauled him to his feet and slammed him against the Dumpster again.

"Here comes the sun," she said with forced levity. "You're toast."

In the distance sirens began to wail. Buffy glanced over at the back door of The Fish Tank and saw eyes—human eyes—watching from within. The door was open four or five inches, but when she looked over it was slammed shut.

The sirens grew closer.

The last thing she wanted was to have to answer questions. There was no time to haul the vampire down the street and hoist him on to a roof. Buffy felt a dark anger rising inside her, but she shook it off. Nothing to be done about it. Plus it wasn't like she could baby-sit the thing all night and still make it to class in the morning.

"Last chance," she told the vampire. "Final Jeopardy. Can't ya just hear that theme in the background?"

His orange, feral eyes sparkled with cold fire, unafraid.

Buffy dusted him.

"So much for saving Giles some research," she muttered.

The corpse of the vampires' victim was sprawled against the back of The Fish Tank with her Aerosmith T-shirt rucked up under her arms. Buffy knew she was dead but she knelt down beside her and felt for a pulse. She couldn't walk away without checking. But there was nothing, of course.

The sirens screamed closer.

Buffy got up and began to sprint away from the scene, along the backs of the buildings where other trash bins awaited pickup. At the end of the block she paused and glanced back. Blue lights swirled in the drive. Police cars roared up the narrow way usually reserved for garbage trucks. Buffy rounded the corner and the lights disappeared behind her.

She slipped her stake back into its sheath. Earlier she had been cold, but now she was too warm, so she unzipped her sweatshirt and tied it around her waist. A bell rang on a buoy out on the ocean and the salt air felt good, invigorating.

When Buffy at last lay her head upon her pillow, sleep would not come. Every time she closed her eyes she could see those burning orange eyes and feel powerful hands upon her throat, the drain of the life force within her. Her mind whirled as she thought about this new breed of vampires. Their tattoos and attributes unified them. They were a single unit, not a group of individual scavengers. She would have to talk to Giles the next day, get to work on figuring out what she was up against.

At last, exhausted, Buffy drifted off to sleep, and she dreamed.

She dreamed she was back in Docktown. . . .

Orange eyes blazed in the shadow of every alley. Buoy bells echoed up from the wharf, where the surf rattled wooden timbers and crashed against the sea wall. A chill breeze whistled through cracked windows in a darkened storefront off to her left and whipped bits of trash along the street. An empty beer bottle rolled along the pavement with a tinkling of glass like mournful wind chimes.

Buffy quickened her pace. They were not attacking, the beasts in the shadows, but she did not like their eyes upon her. They made her feel weak, skittish, like an animal about to bolt into traffic. . . .

When she looked up, her path was blocked by a ghost.

Buffy recoiled, prepared to defend herself, her heart beating wildly. But in a single eyeblink, she relaxed again. It was a ghost in front of her, that much was true. But this particular phantom bore her no ill will. In fact, the dead woman whose spirit drifted intangible and translucent before her had been a Slayer herself centuries before.

"Lucy?" Buffy stared at her, stunned.

The spirit of Lucy Hanover now walked the ghost roads, the pathways between the world of the flesh and the hereafter, helping lost souls find their way to their ultimate destinations. She had aided Buffy sev-

eral times, but usually appeared to Willow, apparently somehow in tune with Willow's magick.

"I come with a warning, Buffy Summers," the ghost said, her voice a wisp, like dry leaves rustling in the breeze. "In my journeys I have come upon the soul of an ancient seer. The Prophet tells of horrible events about to take place."

Through the ghost's shimmering form Buffy could see the street beyond, a Dodge up on blocks, a dog on a rusted chain that ran toward the street and began to bark. At the dog's alarm, Buffy glanced around, hoping the police would not hear and come to investigate.

But she knew there would be no police. She knew this was a dream. With the Slayer, however, a dream was rarely just a dream. Though it took place upon the dreamscape, Lucy's visitation was all too real.

The sound of the surf crashing beneath the docks nearby almost drowned out Lucy's words, so soft were they.

"It will be your fault," the ghost said.

"What's that mean?" Buffy asked. "What will be?"

"I cannot be more specific as yet. I will search for The Prophet again and see if her vision has grown clearer. Until then, I can only say be wary of all that you do and of all the dark forces gathering around you."

The ghostly Slayer shimmered again and then dissipated altogether, first into what looked like static on a television or spatters of rain on the windshield, and then Lucy was simply gone.

Buffy stared at the space where she'd been. The dog kept barking.

Her eyes fluttered open, but only for a moment. An abiding sense of dread had been planted within her, and it lingered in the back of her mind even as she fell back to sleep.

"Great. Thanks," she muttered as she drifted off again. "That was very helpful."

Yet it was not the last dream she would have that night.

Nor the worst.

CHAPTER 2

uffy."

In the dream, she slept in Angel's arms, by a blaze he had set to burn in the enormous stone fireplace at the mansion. Though she knew that his embrace was all of him that she might ever hope to enjoy, still his strong arms around her gave her a deep and abiding sense of contentment. Of peace. It was a peace that her waking hours never afforded her, particularly not of late.

Bliss.

Yet bliss quickly gave way to a kind of dark suspicion. Her sleeping face creased with a frown. There was a malignant presence attempting to worm its way into her mind, to draw her from Angel's tender caress into a world of chaos and horror and sadness.

"Buffy!"

It reached for her, icy grip on her bare shoulder, the warmth from the fire leeched away in an instant. Buffy shook her head, tried to deny the creature's power. She glanced at Angel, but he slept on unaware that she was being attacked, that she was being taken from him.

"No!" she cried, and flinched away from the thing's frozen touch. The Slayer lashed out with a powerful backhand. . . .

"No!" Buffy snapped, as she sat upright in bed, eyes barely open, vision fogged by the remnants of dream. Thoughts slipped slowly back into place in her mind, as though tearing away cobwebs that had been spun there while she slept.

Once, twice, Buffy blinked. Her knuckles stung with the echo of a blow she had landed only a moment ago. She glanced down at her hand and then, horror mounting in her chest, turned to her right, where her best friend and roommate, Willow Rosenberg, sat holding a hand over a growing welt on her face. Willow's eyes were wide with shock, her mouth open in a little "o" that would have been comical under other circumstances.

"Oh God, Will," Buffy muttered groggily. "Oh . . . I was . . . I was dreaming. I'm sorry."

Willow frowned and rubbed her cheek. "That's the last time I try waking you up." With a frustrated sigh she grabbed a light sweater off the back of her desk chair and began to slip it on.

"Are you okay?" Buffy asked. She climbed out of bed and pushed her sleep-wild hair away from her face. "I just . . . I don't know what happened. I was having this dream and I guess you waking me was part of it, but in the dream you were this horrible monster that wanted to . . ."

While Buffy had been talking Willow had gone to the mirror in their room and begun gingerly to touch the still-growing red welt on her left cheek. Willow winced when she poked at it a bit too hard. When Buffy, horrified by what she had done, stopped speaking to watch, Willow turned to face her.

"Your alarm went off a bunch of times. You hit the snooze. Then you turned it off. That was half an hour ago. Since you have class in, like"—she glanced at her watch—"seven minutes, I figured I'd better wake you up. You said you couldn't afford to miss it."

Buffy's mouth opened, but no words came out. She shook her head and let out a long breath. "I really am sorry, Will. I was out really late on patrol last night. Guess I just got carried away with the sleep thing. Can I make it up to you?" she asked brightly. "Mochaccinos on me?"

For a moment longer Willow's grumpy expression remained. Not that Buffy blamed her for it. Then, suddenly, it dissipated as if it had never been there, though the welt remained. Willow offered her patented shy, half-smile and rolled her eyes slightly.

"After last class this afternoon. I want lots of whipped cream. I'm so weak." She sighed. "I've got to have more practice at staying mad."

Buffy offered a sympathetic nod. "It's not your

fault. I didn't play fair. The mochaccinos are like Willow-kryptonite."

"They do drain my resolve," Willow agreed. "That's the problem with fighting with your friends. Devastating knowledge of your vulnerabilities."

"Exactly why we shouldn't do it. Nobody wins."

Willow flashed a sunny grin at that, then winced with the pain it caused, a hiss escaping through her lips.

"Oh, Will," Buffy said quickly, moving toward her. "It hurts that bad? I hope I didn't crack your cheekbone or something. Let's have a look."

They moved together to a half-open window where Buffy could get a good look at Willow's face in the sunlight. Already the swelling had gone down just a tiny bit, but the redness was quickly being replaced by a dark purplish bruise that was certain to draw attention Willow would likely rather do without.

A cool breeze slipped through the window and Buffy shuddered a little.

"It looks pretty bad. Sure you don't want to cover it up? I've got a pretty heavy base you could use."

Willow shook her head sadly. "No time. Besides, that'd kinda make it look even more like the battered-spouse special, don't you think? I don't want anyone thinking I have something to hide. That'd look pretty sad for me, and even worse for Oz."

"Oz," Buffy repeated, and cringed. "He's gonna kill me."

"You marked his girl," Willow told her with grave resignation. Then she nodded firmly. "I'll talk to him.

See if I can keep him from putting that hit out on you. Anyway, a sparkly new glamour oughta cover it up, I just need some time to do it. Meaning after class. Speaking of which, hello, class? You're a brand-new Buffy, remember? Supergirl. You should get going."

Panic swept through Buffy. The next couple of days were going to be a true test of her resolve about juggling her life. Not only did she have a history exam tomorrow, but a research paper due for soc class on Monday. Now on top of that, and keeping up with her classes, a new crew of nasties were in town to complicate things.

Sometimes she felt like Jekyll and Hyde, Buffy and the Slayer, with one persona taking over and pretty much screwing things up for the other. Accidentally slugging her best friend was a perfect example. But Buffy knew if she worked at it hard enough, she could maintain the balance.

"I'm gonna be a little late," she said. "Professor Blaylock will be annoyed, but I've got to call Giles. There's new talent in town, and I want to figure out what I'm up against."

Willow nodded, concerned. "We'll go over there after mochaccinos this afternoon. Research mode is just a flick of a switch away."

"I got it, really," Buffy said quickly. "You've got other things to worry about."

"So do you," Willow reminded her. Then she shrugged. "I'm here when you need me."

"Thanks. Just give me a second."

She called Giles's number, then grimaced with frustration as the machine picked up. "Giles," she said, "it's me. Patrol was kinda crazy last night. We should talk. I'll try again later."

With a sigh, she put down the phone. Willow watched her impatiently. Quickly as she could, Buffy pulled on a heavy wool jersey and blue jeans. Frantic, she poked around her bureau until she found an elastic to tie back her hair.

"Y'know, after Kathy, kinda wondering if maybe you're not cut out for the whole roommate thing," Willow suggested, one eyebrow arched mischievously.

She was joking. That much was clear. The roommate Buffy had been stuck with at the beginning of freshman year had been as aggravating as they came, a total spoiled brat with bad taste in music and zero social skills. She'd also been a demon, but that was another story.

"You're a riot, Will. Thanks a lot," she said dryly. A smirk touched the corners of her mouth as she sat on the bed to put her shoes on. "Okay, I'm in and out at all hours, but I think I'm a pretty good roommate. And you're not exactly perfect yourself. Wet towels on the rug, CDs all over the place, and never mind the studying. You're up so late cracking the books all the time that I'm getting a total inferiority complex. I mean, Kathy had the whole demon excuse. What's yours?"

When Willow didn't respond, Buffy looked up to find her best friend staring at her with a hurt expression on her face. Hurt that gave way to a deep, angry frown.

"I never said I was perfect."

"Hey. I was just teasing," Buffy said. But suddenly she was not certain of that. A part of her had been very serious about the things she said. They had only come out because she was tired and on edge, but now she couldn't take them back.

She went to Willow and placed a hand on the other girl's shoulder. "Really," she promised.

Willow nodded. "I know. We're both sleep deprived, which brings on the crankies, and trying to figure out the wacky world of college. I feel all sitcom couple-y, but maybe you should try to leave the stress of work at the office. We've got heapin' helpings here already."

Buffy sighed with relief. "Deal. Let me just brush my teeth, then we can take off."

"If it's okay with you, I'm going to go on ahead," Willow replied, heading for the door. "I don't want to be late for class."

"Oh," Buffy said softly. "Okay."

Willow went out without another word and closed the door behind her. Buffy stared at the door for a long moment, playing back the scene in her head. Willow had brushed it off, but Buffy knew the things she had said must have hurt. A punch in the face she could forgive, but half-serious comments about her behavior as a roommate had gotten under her skin. Buffy didn't understand it. She just hoped that over the course of the day Willow would forget about it.

They were best friends. In it together, no matter what.

Meanwhile, the clock was ticking and she was already three minutes late for class.

Professor Blaylock's sociology class was held in the Bibeau Social Science Building, in an auditorium with seating for more than two hundred. It was a popular class, and he was a popular teacher. Fortunately for Buffy, that meant that it was usually possible, when late, to sneak in through the back door of the auditorium, wait for Blaylock to turn toward one of the large blackboards on the wall, and then slip into a seat before he noticed.

She had been late a lot the first couple of weeks, but Blaylock had only caught her once.

Buffy slipped in through the door and went halfway up the short stairway that led up to the back of the auditorium. A thick-necked guy with a crewcut and a nose that looked as though it had been broken at least once glanced down at her and smiled conspiratorially. A football player, she thought. It was not the first time she had noticed him, but they had never spoken.

The guy held up a finger to caution her, his eyes on the front of the auditorium. Buffy could hear Professor Blaylock talking about "the epidemic of depression in America," which she thought might well be his favorite subject. He veered off into manic-depression and the sound of his voice changed as though he had turned away. Buffy glanced expectantly at the football player, who looked over and nodded with a grin.

As surreptitiously as possible, Buffy went up the last few steps and jostled her way past three people, headed for the nearest seat in the last row, right next to Mr. Football.

"Well, well, hello there!"

Buffy froze.

The voice belonged to Professor Blaylock.

Embarrassed, she turned to regard him, all the way down at the front of the auditorium. He had his hands on his hips and he was smiling amiably.

"Sorry," Buffy said sheepishly. She shrugged, then gestured toward her seat. "I'll just—"

"No, no, remain standing, please."

Buffy blinked, surprised, then just stood there awkwardly as every student in the auditorium stared at her, most of them with smirks on their faces.

"Your name, please? I'm sorry I can't keep track of all of you."

"Buffy," she said quickly.

"I'm sorry, speak up, please." He was still smiling, but she realized now that there was no humor in it.

"Buffy Summers," she said, a bit snippily now, as anger replaced embarrassment.

"Ah, yes, Miss Summers. Might I presume that your tardiness is due to a last minute's bit of diligence on your research paper?"

A deep frown creased Buffy's forehead. "Well, yeah. I mean, I'm still working on it."

Professor Blaylock's smile disappeared completely. "Still working on it? Which I take it means that you're not prepared to hand it in at this time?"

Buffy blanched. Her mouth went dry. They were all still staring at her, but some of the smiles were gone. Now their expressions were more like the pitiful glances people gave accident victims as they drove by a crash site.

"The paper's not due until Monday. I . . . I wrote it down."

"Then you wrote it down wrong," Blaylock replied coldly.

For the first time she saw the three large multicolored piles of plastic folders on the lecture table at the front of the hall. In the first row, she saw the professor's two teaching assistants turn to look at her with sympathy. Ironically, that made her feel worse.

"I guess I must have," she said so quietly that she was not sure if he heard her. Not that it mattered.

"I guess you must have," Blaylock repeated, not quite mocking her. "You know, Miss Summers, if you had been on time to class today, it might not bother me so much that you don't have your paper. But I find myself disinclined to believe that this was a simple error on your part."

That made her angry again. "It was a mistake, Professor."

"Perhaps. Or maybe you think deadlines don't

really apply to you. Either way, you don't have your paper, do you? So here's what we're going to do. You take all the time you need, Miss Summers. Until the end of the semester, if you like."

Buffy blinked, even shook her head a bit. "I'm sorry?"

"You should be," Blaylock told her. "But, let's move on, shall we? You may deliver the paper whenever you like, Buffy. But for each weekday that passes, you will lose ten points. The weekend you may have off. As of midnight tonight, Wednesday, you will begin with a ninety. Midnight tomorrow, an eighty, and Monday, a seventy. If you should decide to surrender, take your lumps, and simply never deliver the paper, I guarantee you will fail this course.

Buffy could only stare at him.

"Now you may sit."

Mochaccinos with Buffy had been a huge disappointment for Willow. After her last class of the day let out that afternoon, Willow had walked with her to the Espresso Pump and did her best to keep things relaxed and fun. It was supposed to be a best friend thing, a just-girls thing. But Buffy had been so ticked off by her soc professor's humiliating her, and so frustrated with herself, that it had been a tense, awkward hour together.

Willow had tried to tell her that it was an honest mistake, that anyone might have made it. But Buffy was being so hard on herself lately, holding herself to such an impossible standard, that nothing Willow said seemed to make her feel any better.

It killed Willow not to be able to help.

If she's so set on doing everything herself, what does she need me for? Willow thought sadly.

But it wasn't only sadness that she felt. As she walked across campus to the house Oz shared with some other students, she was frustrated and angry as well. Somebody had to have a talk with Buffy. She was pretty sure that somebody was going to have to be her. But unless she could make Buffy listen, it would do no good. And the truth was, nobody could really *make* Buffy do anything.

With a wince of pain, she touched the bone-deep bruise on her cheek and sighed.

Troubled, she rapped on the front door of the house where Oz lived. It was opened by a silent, towering guy with whom Willow had never exchanged a word and who bore the peculiar name of Moon. Not that, as a girl dating a guy named Oz who also happened to be a werewolf, she had any real problem with peculiar, but she kinda thought a housemate named Moon was more than a little ironic, all things considered.

"Hey," she said, by way of greeting and thank you.

Moon raised his eyebrows and shook a finger at her, though whether in welcome or disapproval she did not know. Then he walked off, leaving Willow to find her way upstairs on her own. In his room Oz sat on the floor with a fat-bellied acoustic guitar on his lap, working a complicated series of chords that were proof that he was a more talented musician than he would ever admit.

"Hey," Willow said softly as she entered the room.

Oz glanced up and grunted in surprise. His normally impassive face twitched enough that Willow could almost have said he had made an expression. Not that he *never* made expressions—she'd made him smile often enough—it was simply that they were rare.

"Nice shiner." Oz kept strumming but he missed a note as he said it.

"Woke Buffy up this morning. She was having a nightmare, I guess. Not something I'm all aching to do again. And, okay, best friend and all, so I forgave her, right? Kinda part of the gig. But then later she was just so . . . I don't know. Off?"

Oz studied her with great concern.

Willow went and sat on the floor next to him. Oz watched her and began to strum something soft and sweet, a blues riff she'd heard him play before. Just keeping his fingers busy. *He probably doesn't even know he's playing,* Willow thought.

"I mean, I know all this adjusting is hard for her. But, hello? She's not the only one here. Okay, not exactly out on patrol myself every night, or doomed to die in combat with the forces of darkness, so Buffy does get extra credit. That still doesn't mean she has to be so tense."

Willow paused and looked over at Oz, who had

stopped playing. A tiny smile lifted the corners of his mouth.

"You're her best friend," he said.

"I know," Willow replied with a frown. "But it's not that simple."

"Why not?"

Her mouth opened, but no words came out. Grumpily, Willow narrowed her gaze and stared at him. Then she sighed.

"I know, I know. That means I have to be the cutter of much slack. Which I do! Often! And . . . in this case, maybe not so much. Yes, I'm kinda irked. And not just about the bruise. But I'm also worried. She's putting too much pressure on herself. Superman's got the whole superhero/Clark Kent thing pretty much down, but, hello, comic book character!"

"Next you'll tell me Santa's not real."

"You mock," Willow said grimly, "but I'm serious. I'm guessing this whole Martha Stewart perfection kick is backlash after high school. It must be freaking her out that she has so little control over her life. Even this morning, she's got something cooking . . . 'cause I can always smell something Slayerish cooking . . . but she doesn't want to let anyone in. She has to handle it all herself. Part of the brand-new Buffy mantra. She must feel so alone."

Oz's features were deeply serious now. "But she's not alone," he said.

"No," Willow agreed. "She's not. Which, granted,

is a warm and fuzzy thought, but how do I prove that to her?"

"Maybe you can't," Oz suggested. "Maybe it's something she has to learn on her own."

In the narrow cubbyhole that the woman who had rented him his apartment had deemed a kitchen, but which he had thought looked more like the galley compartment of an airplane, Rupert Giles opened the oven to peek in at the meal he was cooking. The air in the apartment was thick with the rich scents of dinner, and he smiled to himself and hummed a snatch of The Who's "Going Mobile."

Giles opened the refrigerator and reached in to touch the two bottles of Piesporter he had chilling, and was pleased to find them suitably cold. He fished about within and retrieved a block of brie, then pulled a box of crackers down from a cabinet. As he was arranging them on a plate, the doorbell buzzed.

"Hmm?" Giles muttered. He blinked and glanced at the clock on the stove. It was barely half past five, and it was quite unlike his guest to be early.

Curious, he crossed the living room and opened the door. Buffy stood on the welcome mat, the dark canvas bag she carried weapons in slung over one shoulder, and a bemused expression on her face.

"Good evening, Buffy," he said pleasantly. "What exactly do you find amusing?"

She shook her head slowly, her grin widening. "The clothes *do* make the man."

Giles glanced down at himself. He'd dressed casually but with style, as always. *What does she find so . . .*

He blushed slightly. The apron that hung around his neck and was tied behind his back bore a full color image of an enraged Daffy Duck, above which were printed the words "You Want Dinner When?"

"Looks like you're expecting company," Buffy went on. "Is that why you haven't called me back?"

Giles blinked. "Sorry? You called?"

"Five times."

Troubled, he glanced across the apartment at a small corner table in the living room. An old black phone sat by an answering machine that was practically an antique. He had placed a potted plant on the table as well, and the phone and machine were partially obscured.

"I'm terribly sorry," he said as he strode across the room toward the phone. "I was out at the store early this morning, and I've been a bit distracted today. But I'm not deaf. Five times is a bit of an exaggeration, yes?"

Even as he spoke, he slid the potted plant aside and saw the red light blinking on the machine, right next to the number *5*.

"Five times," Buffy repeated.

With a muttered apology, Giles turned toward her and shrugged. "Either your timing was pitiful, or I'm even more distracted than I thought."

"Maybe both," Buffy suggested, smiling softly. Then her smile disappeared. "What time's your company arriving?"

Even as she spoke, Giles detected a hint of something in her voice.

"Not for a little while yet," he assured her. "Olivia's coming in for a few days and I've got dinner on, but I'm perfectly capable of talking and cooking simultaneously."

Buffy hesitated. "Don't want to cramp your style."

"By all means, cramp away," he told her as he stood aside and let her enter. "That didn't come out quite right."

"I get it," Buffy said, her tone quite droll. She walked into the living room and slid into the most comfortable chair. "So what are you cooking for your sweetie?"

Giles blinked. "Well, I'm not sure she quite qualifies as my 'sweetie,' but I've made a chicken cobbler she particularly likes."

Buffy stared at him.

"It's . . . well, it's a bit chilly out, and Olivia's never been shy about her appetite, so I thought—"

With a sigh, Giles folded his arms and sat on one arm of the sofa. He regarded her coolly, though quite aware that his cool was somewhat mitigated by the infuriated cartoon duck emblazoned on his chest.

"Now then. We've got trouble, I assume?"

Buffy's expression changed, darkened, as she considered the question. "With a capital 'T,' " she admitted. "I don't know if it's anything really major. Nothing that screams apocalypse or anything. Just kinda weird and I thought, y'know, that you could do some research."

Giles listened carefully to her recounting of her adventure of the previous evening, including the dream visit from Lucy Hanover. When Buffy was still taking orders from the Watchers Council, he had been her Watcher. They had both long since severed ties with the Council, Giles by their choice, Buffy by her own. Yet though she was no longer officially his responsibility, Buffy had come to mean a great deal to him. He might not be her Watcher any longer, but he still considered himself her mentor as well as her friend. She rarely needed him to provide physical backup for her any longer, but the Slayer still needed counsel, and information.

"These vampires are interesting."

"Meaning creepy and a little upsetting?" Buffy prodded.

"Hmm? Oh, yes, precisely that. It's not like anything I'm familiar with. If they hadn't drained that poor woman I'd be wondering if they were truly vampires at all. The energy sap you felt, and the burning eyes, sound a lot more like a demon than a vampire. I'll begin my research with those attributes, and also concentrate on their tattoos. Perhaps they belong to an order or brotherhood that requires it. It may even be the mark of their master, this Camazotz they mentioned.

"The dream you had about Lucy Hanover may or may not be connected. Either way, her coming to you like that is unusual. I imagine she must have had a powerful reason for doing so, and yet her message seems so oblique, so—"

"Annoyingly vague?" Buffy offered.

"Yes, actually," Giles admitted. "You should be extra wary in the coming days. We all should. Perhaps these vampires you met last night are the threat the ghost warned you about. This Camazotz—"

"I got a feeling there were more of them," Buffy interrupted. She shuddered a bit at the memory of the bat-faces. "A lot more."

"I won't doubt your intuition," Giles told her. He thought for a moment. "Camazotz. That does sound familiar, though I can't fathom where I've heard it before. And I really don't understand these tattoos you mentioned. Popular culture links bats to vampires, but as you well know that is only myth."

"Maybe they've seen too many movies," Buffy suggested.

Giles nodded slowly. "Anything is possible."

"I was joking," Buffy said gravely.

He raised an eyebrow, about to chide her, when the odor of burning pastry reached his nostrils.

"Oh Lord, the cobbler!"

In his frenzied rush to the kitchen, Giles rapped his knee on the coffee table and barked in pain. When he whipped open the oven and reached in, the pot holder slipped slightly in his hand and his thumb touched the baking dish. He hissed and put the dish down on the counter, where it promptly began to burn the Formica.

Giles cursed loudly as he slipped a pair of pot holders under the cobbler, too late to save the counter or his poor thumb. He ran it under lukewarm water, then stuck it into his mouth and began to suck on it. Then he remembered Buffy.

He looked up to see her watching him with an alarmed expression.

"How bad is it?" she asked.

Embarrassed, Giles plucked his thumb from his mouth. "Stings, but I'll be all right."

"I meant dinner. Is it salvageable?"

He studied the brown crust on top of the cobbler, then used a fork to break it open. "I think I'll be able to manage, yes. If I can just get some of this burnt part off the top before Olivia—"

The doorbell buzzed.

Giles closed his eyes and sighed.

"Know what?" Buffy said brightly. "I'm gonna go. Patrol. City that never sleeps, and all that? Maybe I'll find some more bat-face guys and I can, I don't know, take a picture or something for you. And . . . so . . . you'll look into this Camazotz guy?"

"Yes. Get the door, would you?"

"No rush or anything," Buffy told him.

"I'll take care of it. I'll call when I've got something."

Buffy had reached the door. She opened it to find a surprised-looking Olivia on the other side. Giles mustered the best smile he could manage, then remembered the apron and quickly tore it off and tossed it across a chair.

"Olivia, hey," Buffy said. "Just leaving. You guys

have a nice night." She smiled at Giles. "Have fun, you two."

Then she was gone, pulling the door shut behind her. Giles looked at Olivia. She had just come off a plane from London, and yet she seemed perfectly put together as always, in dark pants and an ivory top that seemed to make her cocoa skin even more lustrous. Her sweet smile warmed him, and he let out a long sigh.

"You're a sight for sore eyes," he told her.

"You're not so bad yourself," Olivia replied with a mischievous grin. She went to him and slipped her arms behind his back, lifting her mouth to be kissed.

He obliged.

"I'm afraid I've made a bit of a mess of dinner," Giles confessed.

Olivia's eyes sparkled. "Dinner can wait, Rupert."

Xander didn't hear the knock at first. He was sprawled on the floor in front of the television with his fist stuffed into a tub of Planters Cheese Curls. The tape in the VCR was a bootleg Hong Kong action movie called *God of Gamblers,* with the too-cool-for-the-room Chow Yun-Fat in the title role. His mind was occupied with the task of reading the English subtitles that ran in yellow print across the bottom of the screen, so his visitor had to knock a few times before it caught his attention.

With a frown, he glanced up at the door, then back to the television, and he tried to pretend the knock had been in his imagination. Then it came again and he was forced to push himself up from the floor and amble to the door with his hand still stuffed into the Cheese Curls.

"Don't wanna sign up for your new religion," he muttered at whoever stood on the other side of the door. "Don't want to buy steak knives or encyclopedias."

Of course, since the door in question was around the back of the house and led into the apartment he'd set up in his parents' basement after high school graduation, he knew that whoever was out there wasn't some door-to-door salesman. Which saddened him in a way, as he had for an instant secretly prayed that he would open the door and find Girl Scouts out there.

For the cookies, of course. *'Cause, okay, Girl Scouts, pretty much jailbait,* he thought.

Cheese Curls clutched to his chest, Xander pulled open the door. There was nobody out there.

"Hello?"

He stepped out onto the cement stoop and glanced around just in time to see Buffy heading back toward the front of the house. She turned at the sound of his voice and smiled when she saw him.

"Hey, Xand."

"Buffy, hey. To what do I owe the ecstasy?"

"Just hadn't seen my bud in a while and thought I'd come by, see if you wanna do bump-in-the-night patrol with me tonight."

Xander blinked and stared at her. Back in high school, he and Willow and Buffy had been inseparable, formed the core of what he'd playfully dubbed "The

Scooby Gang." They hung around at the Bronze, they hung around in the school library, they hung around in cemeteries. But with college, things had changed. Xander had come out decidedly against anything resembling more school, even though Willow, Buffy, and Oz had gone on to U.C. Sunnydale. The Scooby Gang still existed, particularly in a crisis, but they did a whole heck of a lot less hanging around than they used to. Buffy just dropping by for a one-on-one visit, and asking him to go on patrol, was a bit out of the ordinary.

"Xander?" Buffy prodded, a frown creasing her forehead.

"Sorry," he replied with a shake of his head. "Brain not able to multitask, and I'm having a hard time not making sexual innuendos surrounding the phrase bump-in-the-night."

"Got it." She bounced a bit on the balls of her feet, crackling with what Xander thought of as good old let's-kill-something Slayer energy. "So, patrol?"

Still curious, but happy to be asked, he rubbed his chin in a way he hoped would imply actual contemplation. "Hmm, let me see. Eat tasty snacks in front of beautifully orchestrated Hong Kong action, or get a little exercise, witness it firsthand, and put my life in mortal jeopardy." He shrugged. "Don't ever quote me, but for some reason only my therapist would understand, I think I'll take mortal jeopardy for a hundred, Alex."

Buffy seemed puzzled. "No mention of Anya."

"Out spending money on girl fashions. She said it

was a gender imperative. Whatever that is." He nodded back toward his apartment. "Let me just grab a jacket."

Nearly two hours had passed without any sign of supernatural presence. Buffy had begun to grow discouraged, but she was still more than a little curious about the bat-faced vampires from the night before. The last thing she wanted was to go home empty-handed, particularly since Giles wasn't exactly on fire with the research at the moment. Of course, she could have asked Willow to get started on it—was actually feeling kind of guilty about not doing so—but when they'd met for mochaccinos earlier, Buffy had felt a bit of tension between them. A kind of distance. She didn't like that at all.

Willow was her best friend. She ought to be able to speak her mind if something was bothering her. But, then again, Buffy hadn't exactly spoken up earlier. Both of them had sort of just let the tension drift until Buffy had taken off for Giles's, worried that he still was not answering his phone.

As soon as she got back to the dorm that night, Buffy vowed to talk to Willow, dispel the weirdness that had been between them since that morning. Meanwhile, she deeply regretted having invited Xander to come on patrol with her.

What the hell was I thinking?

But she knew the real reason she had asked Xander along. With Giles occupied by Olivia, and with the awkwardness she felt with Willow at the moment,

Buffy needed someone around to reassure her that she wasn't just the Slayer.

Though she and Xander had patrolled around the Bronze and through the major cemeteries, Buffy had rushed through it and drifted west toward the ocean. There were some very nice neighborhoods near the beach, but they were not her target. She certainly did not expect to find the tattooed vampires back at The Fish Tank again, but once the major hunting grounds turned up empty she decided to sweep the wharf area again. Xander complained about his feet and about the distance, but not very much. It seemed to Buffy that half the time he only brought it up to give them something to talk about, to remind her that he was there.

If it had been earlier, she probably would have pretended to bail on patrol and walked him home, then come back out by herself. He made her laugh, of course. Xander was always good for that. Made her feel like herself, just another nineteen-year-old girl. But that was only on the surface. Underneath, she worried for him, and felt guilty for having dragged him along just to mark "hanging out with friends" off the checklist in her head.

But it would be okay, she told herself. That pressure was part of balancing her life.

She refused to let Professor Blaylock's humiliating her, or the research paper that still hung over her head, or even the exam she had in the morning, shatter her focus.

Focus. That was what it was all about.

The temperature had dropped considerably in the hours after dusk, and she shuddered despite the heavy wool jersey she wore over her shirt. Xander turned up the collar of his jacket. Buffy rotated her head and a muscle in her neck popped, releasing some of the tension she felt. The canvas bag over her shoulder was a minor annoyance, but worth it for the crossbow she carried inside it. Xander had a couple of stakes she had given him stuck in the pockets of his dark brown jacket. Together they walked down a deserted sidewalk in a block of run-down apartments that ended with a gas station on the corner.

Across the street from the gas station was a dingy-looking Italian place called Maria's that Buffy suspected might be Mafia-owned. Next to that was a tattoo parlor, and on the other side of that, the Kat Skratch Club. It was an ugly-looking place with a lot of neon in the window and on the sign, but a layer of grime seemed to sit over the whole thing. A blinking string of letters in the window promised "Live Girls," which Buffy appreciated, considering the not-so-unrealistic alternative was dead ones. The Kat Skratch had topless dancers 365 days a year, according to a hand-painted sign in one window that they spotted as they crossed the street toward it.

"Maybe we should stop in, rest our feet, grab a . . . mineral water or something?" Xander suggested.

Buffy shot him a doubtful glance and Xander put on his wide-eyed-innocence face and shrugged in return.

"Why'd you bring me?" he asked suddenly.

Buffy was surprised by the earnest expression on his face. She would have asked what he meant by the question, but she didn't want to play coy woman with him. Just wouldn't be fair.

"I'm not allowed to miss you?" she asked.

"You're not allowed, you're required," he told her archly. "But there's more going on. You could've asked Willow. Or Giles. Not that I'm anything less than battle-ready at all times. Xander Harris and his fists of fury await the call of combat. But . . . there's a but. You can feel it in the air. A but. So what's the but?"

Buffy nodded slowly and sighed. Then she shot him a hard look. "I do miss you, though."

"Understood."

"I kind of had a fight with Willow. And, y'know, I'm all about the learning now. Got an exam in the morning and I'm pretty much ready. How often can I say that? But I blew a major deadline in my soc class today and I don't even know how it happened. I mean, I'm totally on top of things. Except, apparently, this."

Xander smiled. "You've got a jam-packed life, Buffy. It's gonna get messy sometimes."

Buffy stared. "I can't afford to have it get messy anymore, Xander. Sometimes I feel like Buffy's going to disappear and then there'll just be the Slayer left."

"Not as long as I'm around. That's what your friends are for." Xander's smile disappeared after a moment and he studied her with great seriousness. "Speaking of, what's up with Willow?"

For a moment Buffy tried to find the words to explain not only her argument with Willow, but her feelings about it. Then she glanced over at the front door of the Kat Skratch Club and saw three men and a woman shoving and laughing as they spilled out onto the sidewalk.

All four of them had bats tattooed across their eyes.

Buffy reached into her bag.

"Hold that thought."

CHAPTER 3

"Wow, you let girls in the club, too? I wish you'd told me, so I could get a goofy tattoo on *my* face."

The four bat-faces glared at Buffy. As they did, their eyes began to flare with orange sparks. The female, cinched and draped in black leather like the others, took a step forward and tilted her head with curiosity, eyeing the Slayer up and down. Buffy had dropped the bag in front of the pawn shop and now held the cross-bow in both hands, primed and ready. It was an old-fashioned Chinese model, a repeater, able to shoot six bolts with only a couple of seconds between them.

"What are you supposed to be?" the female asked, an expression of amusement on her face. Her fore-head and the corners of her mouth crinkled and Buffy saw that she had caked white makeup on her face, apparently to make a more striking contrast with the black ink of the bat.

Buffy returned her smirk. "Me? Look in a mirror lately?"

One of the males, a broad-shouldered goon with a face like a bulldog and a chain that ran from his right ear to his nostril, snorted with derisive laughter. His electric eyes blazed brighter.

"You don't know how funny that is," he rumbled in the same weird accent she had heard the night before. Seemed they all had it.

"Actually, I do."

That gave them pause. All four of the vampires regarded her a bit more closely. A dog began to howl down along the block and several took up the cry in response.

It was chilling. Buffy shivered, but she smiled to cover it. She had faced evils older than man, demons whose depravity would make the bravest soldier weep, and had come out on top. Four wannabes with face paint weren't about to rattle her.

Yet in some way, they did. That bat tattoo was part of it. It spoke on an instinctive level to some primal part of her, and a frisson of fear ran through her that she could not blame on howling dogs. But more so, their eyes bothered her, for with that burning energy came her memory of the way the one the night before had sapped her strength. If she had not broken away when she did, she would have been powerless.

Powerless. Nothing frightened her more.

Xander had approached them with her, a good six feet back and over her left shoulder, just where she wanted him. Now she sensed him shifting slightly, perhaps unnerved by the dogs.

"Not sure I like the math here, Buff," he whispered.

The vampires glanced quickly at him, as one, almost like a pack of dogs. One, whose bat tattoo spread its wings almost all the way around his bald head, licked his lips. Then they grinned and turned their attention back to Buffy, and their faces shifted all at once, their fangs protruding from their mouths, their brows growing thicker and more bestial.

"Nobody likes math, Xander," she said, almost under her breath. "But we do it. For instance . . . subtraction."

Buffy lunged.

The vampires rushed her.

"Don't let them touch you!" she snapped at Xander.

With a grunt deep in her chest, right hand holding the crossbow out to one side, Buffy used her left arm to grab the nearest bat-face around the neck and choke him. With her weight on him, she launched a snap-kick high and hard, and the side of her foot caught the bulldog with the nose chain under his jaw. Bulldog crashed backward into the clown-faced girl and they both went down. When she came down, she was still choking the first one that had attacked her. Buffy twisted him around and flipped him onto the pavement. It was a throw her first Watcher, Merrick, had taught her when she was fifteen years old. That was one of the earliest lessons she'd learned as the Slayer. Go with what works.

"Xander!" she shouted.

Even as she turned to defend herself against the bald one, she caught a glimpse of Xander falling upon the one she'd flipped and dusting him with a stake.

Suddenly, Buffy felt a little better. These guys were faster and stronger than other vamps she'd fought, and they seemed to surge with that weird, phosphorescent energy . . . but if Xander could dust one, how tough could they be?

Bulldog was furious at having been knocked on his butt. He had just extricated himself from the clown-faced girl, or was trying to. She bumped into him, cost him a half a second. The bald one rushed Buffy then.

Crossbow held firmly in both hands, she fired a bolt into the vampire's heart, which exploded into dust. The next bolt snapped up into position and she swung the crossbow at Clownface and Bulldog, who froze for just a moment before rabbiting back toward the club. Buffy fired two more bolts before they slammed through the front door of the Kat Skratch, and both of them thunked into Bulldog's back with a wet, tearing noise. He didn't even slow down.

"Happens every time," Xander said as he stepped up beside her. "They see me, they cower in terror and then flee."

"You're a pretty imposing presence," Buffy confirmed. "Really. I think it's the bowling shirt."

Scandalized, Xander glanced down at the blue and

brown shirt he wore beneath his jacket. "Hey, this is very much in style. And, okay, a bit pungent, but Mom's a little behind on the laundry, okay?"

"Your mother stopped doing your laundry when you moved into the basement."

Xander raised an eyebrow. "That explains a lot."

"So," Buffy went on. "Four minus two."

"Equals two. Call me the math whiz. What next?"

Buffy looked at the door to the club. "We keep subtracting."

"Never thought I'd be happy to hear that, but live girls await. Lead on!"

The inside of the Kat Skratch Club was awash with multicolored lights and roiling with music so loud and jarringly discordant that Buffy doubted it could still be called rock 'n' roll. For a place dedicated to the consumption of alcohol and the ogling of half-naked women, nobody seemed to be having a very good time. Bikers and fishermen and dockworkers made up most of the male population of the place . . . which pretty much made up the population of the place. There were very few women there who weren't either onstage or waiting on tables, and Buffy figured most of them were either prostitutes or girls who worked hard at looking like prostitutes.

When she and Xander walked in the bouncer had his back to them, his gaze locked on a girl onstage who wore the remnants of a Catholic-school uniform several sizes too small for her. The bar ran down the entire left wall, and two stages jutted out from the wall on the right. In between there were plenty of tables. Buffy narrowed her gaze against the strobing lights and concentrated enough to cut out most of the music. There was no sign of the vampires, nor any sign that anyone had even noticed them come rushing through.

"Suddenly bump-in-the-night patrol has a whole new meaning," Xander said, voice tinged with awe.

The bouncer heard him. The burly, bearded guy turned to glare at them and his eyes ticked to the crossbow in Buffy's hands, then back to her face. "Only way you're getting in here, girlie, is up on that stage."

"Not that the idea doesn't hold some appeal," Xander told the man, "but you *so* should not have said that."

With a violent twinkle in his eye, the bouncer scoffed and moved toward Xander. "Yeah, weasel? And why not?"

At his most charming, Xander grinned. "Mainly 'cause I'm guessing Lloyd's of London? Not holding an insurance policy on your teeth?"

Just as the burly guy reached for Xander's throat Buffy grabbed the bouncer by the wrist. He winced in pain, stared at her in surprise, then tried to pull away. Buffy held on. He could not break her grip.

"You're not going to touch my friend or me. We're not here to drink. We'll be in and out before you know it. You shouldn't have tried to hurt him."

"You arrogant little—" the bouncer growled, cutting himself off as he threw a punch with his free hand.

Buffy stopped the punch with the stock of her crossbow, then shoved him back, hard. He went down onto the beer-sticky wooden floor without so much as a grunt.

"Five minutes. Then we're gone like we were never here."

The bouncer swallowed once and rubbed his wrist. Then he nodded slowly and began to rise, turning back toward the door to the club. A ripple of angry mutterings went through the club, and onstage two of the girls stopped dancing to stare. A couple of bikers got up from a nearby table and loomed menacingly toward them.

"Sit," Buffy said impassively, as she raised the crossbow to chest level. She would never have shot them with it, of course, but they didn't know that.

They both glanced at the bouncer, then sat down.

"Come on," she said, and then she started weaving through tables, past glaring, thick-necked laborers. Xander muttered something as he followed her, but Buffy paid no attention. They had taken too much time at the door. The vampires were nowhere in sight. That meant either the rest rooms or some other room in the rear. Buffy figured they'd head for a back door, if there was one. She headed for the heavy wooden door at the far end of the bar. None of the lights reached that far, so most of the patrons wouldn't even have noticed the door.

The music kept pummeling the room, the girls started dancing again, and before Buffy and Xander had even reached the door, everyone's attention was back on the girls or their drinks. Buffy held the crossbow at the ready and set herself in a fighting stance, muscles tensed.

"Xander, get the door."

All seriousness now, no trace of amusement on his face, Xander edged up beside her, reached down to turn the knob and shove the door open, then dropped back. Buffy surged forward into what appeared to be a dingy dressing room for the dancers. Lockers and mirrors abounded, but the room was poorly lit. Not so dark, however, that she could not see them.

Bulldog. Clownface. Four . . . no, five others.

Buffy froze just inside the door, blocking Xander's entrance.

"What is it?" he asked anxiously.

"More math." She reached back and handed Xander a stake. He took it. Then Buffy grabbed the door and slammed it shut behind her, leaving him out in the club. Xander shouted her name and she called back to him to stay put.

If there were other vamps out in the club, she doubted they would reveal themselves. But if they did, Xander had the stake. Meanwhile, she had room to work.

The vampires moved in almost total silence across the room, seeming to uncoil from the darkness like serpents. Clownface and Bulldog hung back while the others moved closer. In the near darkness, the

orange fire of their jack-o'-lantern eyes set into the
black inks of the tattoos that were etched across their
faces was unsettling.

They began to chant something, all at once and all
together, in a language Buffy did not recognize. It
was in a kind of deep undervoice almost as though
they were whispering it to themselves. The chanting
slipped under her skin immediately, eerie fingers
trailing along her spine and raising goosebumps on
her arms. Buffy felt her eyes flutter and the lids grow
heavy.

With a surge of anger and adrenaline, she shook
it off.

"You think I'm that easy?" she asked dismissively.

Xander called her name again and pushed open the
door behind her. In a single motion, Buffy spun and
slammed it shut, knocking him back out into the bar-
room, then turned to face the vampires, just as they
swarmed her.

Her finger tightened on the trigger of the crossbow.
A bolt flew, punched through the heart of the vampire
closest to her, and he exploded in a blast of hot ash.
Another bolt ratcheted into place but another vampire, a thin white scar slicing through the markings
on his face, lunged for her throat, his long tongue
slaking out over his fangs. Talons reached for her.
She knew she could not let them get a grip on her.
With a backhand, Buffy slammed her left fist up
under his jaw and caught the vampire's tongue between his teeth.

He screamed in pain and staggered back, clearing Buffy enough room to aim at a third and fire again. The vamp's eyes went wide as the bolt slammed into his ribcage and then through his heart. A second later he was dusted.

"Too quiet," Buffy chided the remaining bloodsuckers. "Vampire mimes, is that it? Let's have heaps of arrogant swagger. You guys love arrogant swagger."

They said nothing. There were still five of them, but Buffy saw Clownface grab Bulldog's arm and hold him back as the other three came for her again, trying to corner her. Buffy had one last bolt in the repeating crossbow. She swung the weapon up just as they all attacked. This time she was not fast enough. The crossbow was batted from her hand with a blow hard enough to make her right hand numb. It clattered to the floor and Buffy heard the wood crack.

"Hey!" she snapped.

One of the vampires pushed the others out of the way, greedy to get at her, and wrapped his talons around her throat, choking off her words and her air. The thing slammed her into a mirror and a rain of shattered glass cascaded across the floor.

Buffy pushed her feet against the wall for leverage and then head-butted the vampire as hard as she could. Her aim was a little off and her skull crushed his nose with a splintering of bone and a spray of blood.

"That bow," she snarled, "was an antique. Giles is not going to be happy. He might even swear."

One of the others came at her from the left. Buffy ducked the blow, leaned back and snapped a kick at the vampire's chest that staggered him.

Another bat-face reached for her, but Buffy was too fast. She reached behind her and withdrew the stake from its sheath at the small of her back, then spun and punched it through his chest. The scarred one with the broken, mashed nose lunged at her through the cloud of his comrade's dust. Buffy swung her right fist in a blow that came up from her gut and he went down hard on the floor.

After that she moved in a single fluid motion. A spinning kick to the face of her remaining attacker was followed by a thrust of the stake, and more dust blew around the room. She dropped to the floor, stake above the scarred one's heart, nose to nose with the vampire. His breath was wretched, the stench of old blood.

Buffy dusted him.

Instantly she was up, turning, body tense and ready for more, wanting combat and, with some luck, answers. She had figured to interrogate the last one alive. But she had not expected them to run away. The last of them, the two she had come to think of as Clownface and Bulldog, were gone, a distant rear door to the club hanging open to the night.

Half a dozen wisecracks came to mind, but none made it as far as her lips. Vampires ran from her all the time, but this was different. There was no doubt in her mind that the two escapees had not run out of cowardice, but as some form of strategic retreat. The idea disturbed her profoundly. The vampire breed was a contentious one and they rarely got along well enough to form alliances, never mind packs or families. Only the most charismatic and powerful like the Master were able to gather followers in that way.

Whoever this Camazotz was, he had trained his acolytes well.

With those dark thoughts in mind, she pulled open the door to the club. Xander leaned against the wall to her left, staring at the two girls on the stage closest to them. It took him nearly ten seconds to notice Buffy standing there watching him.

"Hey. Just on the job. Making sure you're not disturbed," he said nervously.

"My hero." Buffy raised an eyebrow.

Xander balked. "You pushed me out of there. Closed the door in my face not once but twice. Kinda figured that meant I'd just be cannon fodder if I forced my way in. If you needed backup I thought you woulda yelled for me."

"I would have," Buffy agreed. Then she smirked. "Whether or not you would have heard me is another question entirely."

"What?" Xander asked. His eyes strayed to the stage. "Oh, that? Barely noticed them. Just backing you up, Buffy. You will tell Anya it was you who dragged me in here, right?"

Buffy made her way around tables and toward the front door of the Kat Skratch Club amidst clouds of cigarette smoke. None of the patrons even gave her a second glance.

Xander trailed after her. "Buffy? You'll tell her, right?"

CHAPTER 4

The dentist's-drill buzz of the alarm clock woke Buffy at just after seven o'clock the following morning. One eye flickered open and she glared at it with as much hatred as she had ever felt for more corporeal demons. Just looking at the thing would not make it shut off, however, so she was forced to sit up, eyes slitted open, and click it off.

"I hate Mondays," she grumbled under her breath. Of course, it wasn't Monday. But it felt like one.

With a frown, Buffy looked around the room. Willow's bed was still made, unrumpled. Her roommate had not come home the night before. It wasn't unheard of for Willow to spend the night at Oz's, but Buffy could not help but wonder if the brief argument they'd had the day before had anything to do with it.

She was tempted to call Oz, but it was too early. Willow would likely be up already, but you could never tell with Oz. One day he might make all of his classes and the next he might sleep until after lunch.

"No," she told herself sternly. "No grumpy thoughts."

Determined to make a fresh start of the day, she got up and peered out the window. The sky was gray, overcast, but it was almost guaranteed to burn off. It was fall, sure, but it was also Southern California. Bad weather happened, but it was rare enough that nobody believed it until it did some damage, then afterward they pretended it had never been there. Almost exactly the same way the people of Sunnydale dealt with the supernatural.

"No grumpy thoughts," she said again.

Humming a snatch of some tune the Dingoes always played at the Bronze, she got her things together and went down the hall to take a shower.

Fifteen minutes later she was back in her room. Her mind drifted to the run-in at the Kat Skratch Club the night before. The tattoos, the vampires' eerie chanting, their eyes, and their arrogance; much as she hated to admit it, even to herself, they creeped her out.

Giles had promised to do research on Camazotz, and she knew he would get it done as soon as possible. But having Olivia around would complicate things. After the chaos of last night Buffy had been tempted to go back to his apartment and check in, but the idea of interrupting their romantic evening stopped her cold. The last thing she wanted to do was disturb Giles's love life, never mind walk in on it.

Shudder. That thought was creepier than bat-faced vampires.

Buffy glanced at her enemy, the alarm clock. It was a little after seven-thirty, still plenty of time before class, and the desire to call Willow and square things if they needed to be squared lingered with her.

Oz answered. "Yeah?" he rasped.

"Hey, Oz. Sorry to call so early. Is Willow up?"

"Hang on."

A muffled exchange on the other end, then Willow came on.

"Hey."

"Hey. Sorry to bother you guys."

"No bother," Willow said brightly. "At least, not me. But I'm not a cranky old bear in the morning like certain boyfriends. What's up?"

Buffy paused. It would sound silly if she brought up their argument, or just said she was checking in.

"Buffy? You okay?"

"Good," Buffy replied quickly. "No grumpy mornings over here. Listen, there's some interesting new talent in town and I was going to head over to Giles's this afternoon, see what we could dig up. Want to come with?"

"Mmm," Willow replied, sounding a bit distracted. Buffy tried not to be envious that her best friend had a guy who loved her to be distracting. "Why don't we meet you there?"

"Deal. Gotta go, though. Time to make with the book learnin'. Got my history exam this morning. Then I've got to work on that paper for Professor Blaylock. As of today, I'm starting with a ninety."

"Knock 'em dead," Willow said. "Only, y'know, not literally."

They said their good-byes and hung up, and when Buffy left the dorm room she had a broad smile on her face. Willow meant the world to her and Buffy had no idea what she would do if there ever came a day when Willow did not feel the same.

Oz sat cross-legged on the floor of Giles's apartment, excavating ancient treasures from the man's vinyl record collection. Olivia, a woman Willow had only met a time or two before, but who clearly meant a great deal to Giles, sat on a cushioned chair by Oz and exclaimed over a number of the records he pulled out, many of which spurred her to regale them with embarrassing stories of Giles in his younger days.

She was certainly a beautiful woman, and her British accent gave her an added allure. Willow felt badly for having interrupted their time together.

"Are you sure this is okay?" she said, keeping her voice low.

Giles sat beside her at the dining room table as the two of them pored through a stack of arcane texts. A couple of them were even older than the most antique volumes she had previously seen in his collection, and most were in Spanish.

"Giles?" Willow prodded.

He blinked several times, then looked up at her as though he'd just been snapped awake by a hypnotist. "I'm sorry, Willow, what was that? Have you found something?"

"Not yet, no. I just . . . I know you and Olivia don't get to see each other very often. She's not in from London for very long. Are you sure you want to be doing this today?"

Giles removed his glasses and offered her a gentle smile. "It's very sweet of you to be concerned. The answer, of course, is no. I don't want to be doing this at all. But I also realize that lives may be in jeopardy from these new arrivals, and a bit of research is the least I can do to help Buffy in her effort to combat them. She may have decided that she's going to be invincible, but unless someone goes 'round and gets the rest of the world to agree, we must back her up."

He glanced over his shoulder as Olivia laughed about a particular record. Oz said something under his breath. Something ironic, Willow was sure, because he was Oz, after all.

"Oz seems to have Olivia quite well entertained at the moment," Giles reassured Willow. "Though how he manages to do that and maintain his usual twelve-word-an-hour rule is a mystery to me."

"He's a good listener," Willow said, a lopsided smile on her face as she watched her guy. When she smiled, the bruise Buffy had given her the previous morning made her wince. The glamour she'd used could hide it, but not make the pain go away.

"So anything?" she asked Giles.

"Quite a bit, actually." He separated out two of the books from his pile. "I just thought I'd hold off until Buffy arrived to avoid having to explain it more than once."

Troubled, Willow wondered where Buffy had gotten off to. That morning she had asked that they all meet at Giles's after classes were over. Willow knew for a fact that Buffy's last class of the day was out before three o'clock. Now it was going on four and still no Buffy.

"I expected her long before now," Giles added.

It only made Willow more concerned. "I hope she's all—"

She was interrupted by a knock at the door. Willow leaped up from the table to get it. Giles reached for a book he had set aside. Engrossed in the record collection, Oz and Olivia were about to put on an early Rolling Stones album, but they paused to look up.

Willow opened the door to find Buffy standing on the stoop.

"Hey!" Willow said. "You're okay."

"Sorry I'm late. It's just, this paper for Professor Blaylock. I thought I had a lot of this stuff down, but I feel like I'm starting from square one. No way am I going to finish before Monday, which is when it was due in the first place. I'll be starting from a seventy. It'll have to be perfect for me to pass. Then, this afternoon, I run into Aaron Levine, who's in my history class? We got to talking about the exam this morning, which I thought I'd done all right on. Turns out, not so much. I mixed up a couple of royal families, so one of the big essays is written in the language of gibberish. I just don't know what's wrong with me."

Willow frowned, then forced a smile. "Tell you what? You've got the stress. Maybe you'd feel better if you went back and worked on that paper. Let us deal with the mystery for a while. Then, when you feel like you've got a better handle on things—"

"I've got a handle on things now," Buffy snapped.

Surprised by her anger, Willow took a step back. She glanced around the room and saw that everyone was staring at Buffy.

"Except, perhaps, your temper," Giles chided her.

Buffy began to form some sort of retort, but then her features softened. She gazed apologetically at Willow.

"Sorry, Will. Maybe I am wound a little tight right now, with all this. Thanks for worrying about me, but I really can handle it. I *will* handle it."

"Preferably without the crankiness," Willow replied, still a bit hurt.

Buffy put a hand on her shoulder. Willow saw the regret and the stress in her eyes, and wished she could do more to help.

"Hey. Are *we* okay?" Buffy asked.

"Peachy," Willow said with a firm nod. "Without the pit, even."

"We're in a place with fruit," Buffy replied happily. "Gotta like it. As long as we go nowhere near lemons. There's a whole sour element there."

"No lemons," Willow promised.

Giles rose from the table as Buffy approached.

"Sorry for the lustus interruptus," she said, casting a meaningful glance at Olivia, who smiled and waved without the faintest trace of embarrassment.

And why should she be embarrassed, Willow thought. *It's her boyfriend's apartment, they're consenting adults, and we're the intruders here.* On the other hand, with their positions reversed Willow knew that she'd be blushing scarlet and barely able to speak beyond a babble.

"Yes, well, ritual mass murder does tend to take priority over almost anything else," Giles told her.

Buffy cast a sidelong glance at Willow. "See, it's the 'mass' in there that always gets me. I hate vampires with ambition. Why can't they be ambition free?"

In the corner, as he placed the needle on vinyl, Oz spoke without looking up from the antique record player. "Everyone's gotta have a dream."

Giles cleared his throat. "Yes, well, your timing is impeccable as usual, Buffy. I believe we've found what we're looking for."

"We were just waiting for you to get here," Willow said helpfully. "Giles didn't want to repeat himself."

"Sorry I held you guys up."

Giles held up a hand to wave away her apology. "No matter. Let's get down to business, shall we?"

Willow and Buffy sat together on the sofa. Oz left

the Rolling Stones on with the volume low and wandered over. Olivia gazed at them for a moment, then rolled her eyes good-naturedly and went up the stairs into the loft.

Giles gave them all a sheepish glance and shrugged. "Olivia's a skeptic," he told them in a stage whisper. "Thinks we're all a bit mad, I suspect."

"She should spend more time in Sunnydale," Buffy replied. "It'd make a believer out of her."

Oz settled deeply into an old chair. Giles stood before them, leaning only a little against the dining room table, cracked leather book in his right hand.

"According to all the legends I've been able to find, Camazotz was not a vampire, but a god," Giles began.

"Ooh, pagan deities. Have we slain any of those yet?" Willow asked excitedly.

Oz smiled down at her, touched the side of her face. "None of the big ones."

"Camazotz is not exactly a household name," Buffy put in. "I'm guessing he's not one of the big ones, either."

"On the contrary," Giles countered. He opened the book in his hand and flipped to a page toward the end. The paper crackled as he turned the pages. When he held it up for them, Willow saw immediately what he meant for them to see. A drawing in the lower left corner of the page showed a hideous creature like a giant humanoid bat, with prickly fur and pointed ears, long tapered talons and leathery, veined wings. It had a dozen smaller limbs with their own talons protruding from its chest and a thick ratlike tail with what appeared to be a sharp spike at the end.

"According to the ancient Mayans," Giles continued, "Camazotz was the god of bats. He was wed to the dark goddess Zotzilaha Chimalman, and purportedly dwelt in an ancient, tomblike cave that led to a realm of darkness and death. Translated, the name of his lair was simply the House of Bats."

Buffy shifted on the couch. "So we're thinking demon. Tunnel to realms of death sounds like a Hellmouth to me."

"Or," Willow put in quickly, "at least a Hell-nostril."

Everyone looked at her oddly.

"Bad metaphor," she muttered to herself. "Bad, icky metaphor."

Giles turned to slide the tattered old book onto the dining room table. Then he picked up another, smaller volume that was obviously much more recent, though still quite old. When he opened it Willow could see that the text inside had been written by hand and she knew it must be one of the journals kept by the Watchers over the ages.

"The Council let you keep those?" she asked, before she could stop herself.

"Hmm?" Giles glanced up at her and frowned.

Willow wished she had not brought it up. Giles had been fired from the Council because they had felt his relationship with Buffy had become too emotional, that he cared too much for her to be an effective Watcher. He had been angry with them and seemed more than content to cut off all contact, but Willow suspected it was still a sore spot. Still, she had brought it up.

"The journal," she said. "Kinda thought with, y'know, the divorce, that the Council would have asked for those back."

"Ah, yes. Well, Wesley did confiscate most of the handwritten ones I had. I was allowed to keep those that were not originals and this single volume. It was written by my grandmother, who was quite a story-teller, actually. She cataloged many of the odd vampire myths and legends she came across. I thought I remembered something about Mayans in here. If the stories she was told are true, Camazotz was the spawn of a union between a true demon, one of the first to walk the Earth, and a god. What 'god' means in these terms is really anyone's guess, since no one has ever really been able to catalog a meeting with one, to my knowledge.

"Suffice to say, Camazotz is a very ancient creature. Decidedly not a vampire, you understand, but my grandmother notes one particular theory that Camazotz was the demon responsible for the *creation* of vampires."

Buffy slid to the edge of the couch and stared at him. "Can that be true?"

"We have no way of knowing," Giles replied. "Nor have I been able to ascertain, thus far, why his vampire followers should have powers greater than their brethren."

"The god of bats. So the markings on their faces are what, his personal logo?"

"It probably comes from that cave," Willow suggested. "Okay, assuming dark and nasty lair really existed, not much of a stretch to think lots of bats there." She nodded sagely. "I'm thinking maybe he believes his own hype. God of bats. Tattoos the lackeys."

"Or a brand," Buffy said. "Like on cattle. To mark them as his."

Giles seemed to contemplate that for a moment, then held up his grandmother's journal. "The one thing in the journal that reflects the Mayan legends is the idea that Camazotz was the prince of the Mayan legions of darkness, a leader among the creatures of the night. He is a formidable foe."

"That's all we've got? Nothing on the lackeys?" Buffy asked, resignation in her voice. "Sparkly eyes, life-force sucking? Nothing?"

"For the moment I'm afraid that's it," Giles said. "It's possible the draining effect was the sorcery of that particular vampire, but time will tell. Buffy, why don't you—"

"I'll patrol again tonight. See if I can't finally hold on to one of these guys. With the brands on their faces, they're hard to miss. I might swing by Willy's and see if he's got any information for us."

Buffy stood up, tossed her jacket over her shoulder again, and started for the door. While they'd been talking, she'd been relaxed and even joking around.

But Willow saw the change come over her. Suddenly she was all business again, doing it all on her own.

"Will, can you call Xander, ask him and Anya to come by. Giles can brief them. If Anya has any contacts among the demon set that she's still willing to talk to, maybe she can make a few calls. Otherwise you guys should just be checking the paper, airline records, shipping manifests, trying to figure out how they got here and where they could all be staying. That's a lotta new vampires at once. Bigger than a breadbox. My guess is Camazotz will have a Sunnydale version of his House of Bats somewhere. That's something else to check. Where would we find bats around here?"

As Buffy spoke, Willow's eyes widened with alarm and awkwardness. "Um," she countered. "Maybe Oz and I can just go by Xander's. Giles has sort of done his part for the moment."

Buffy glanced up into the loft where Olivia had gone. "Right!" she said quickly. "Absolutely. All done with Giles, at least until the morning. We'll do just fine. Really. We'll check in tomorrow."

Giles busied himself with reorganizing the books on the table as Willow and Oz quickly followed Buffy out.

In front of Giles's apartment, they turned to face each other.

"Sure you don't need any backup on patrol?" Willow asked.

Buffy shook her head. "I've got it. Besides, I'm just going to sweep the regular circuit and swing past the areas where I've seen them before, then I'm going to head back to the dorm early, try to work on that paper and not think about how badly I messed up my history exam."

Willow wanted to reach out to her, to help in some way, but Buffy had been like one big frayed nerve the last few days. Still, she had to try.

"Hey. I know you're hell-bent on handling everything yourself, but everybody needs help sometimes, right? Are you sure you don't want us to round up a posse, go out and pinch-hit for you tonight so you can get that paper in? You could save yourself a whole letter grade. It isn't like we haven't done it before."

Buffy sighed with frustration. "I know that, all right? And it isn't that I don't appreciate it. But you shouldn't have to. It isn't your responsibility, it's mine. I can't keep leaning on you or anyone else. If I'm going to do it myself, I've got to know that I can handle it."

Oz said nothing, only watched the two girls. Willow gazed imploringly at Buffy.

"Your friends are part of this life you're talking about having, Buffy."

Buffy's mouth twitched and a grimace of hurt washed across her features. Then she sighed and her expression hardened.

"You don't understand, Will. But that's okay, really. How can anyone?"

With that, she turned and walked away. Willow stared after her best friend as she disappeared into the darkness, hoping Buffy would turn around, hoping she would see that she could not do it alone.

Willow was about to call after her when Oz put a hand on her arm.

"Let it go."

She gazed at him, not understanding.

"It's hard for her, trying to make it all work," he said.

Willow glanced down, trying and failing to hide her hurt. "It's hard for all of us. Can't she see that it isn't just her? That nobody can deal with everything life throws them if they're all alone?"

"Give it some time. She'll come around," he promised. Then he slipped an arm around her and walked her to his van.

As they drove over to Xander's house, Willow stayed silent, holding her hurt close.

CHAPTER 5

"**W**e got nothing."

With a frown, Giles looked up from the map of Sunnydale that was spread across his dining room table. Xander and Anya sat on the floor in the middle of his apartment with the previous week's local newspapers arranged around them so expansively it appeared as though Giles had bought a puppy that was not yet housebroken.

"Surely there must be something," Giles said, disheartened at Xander's declaration. "A downed plane. Strange stories from the border patrol. Violence at airport customs in Los Angeles. Something to give us just an inkling of where they might have made their lair locally."

Anya gestured with a hand to indicate the newspapers. "Nothing. The new mayor has issued more lies disguised as promises, as expected of the more talented politicians. The Coast Guard is fighting charges they didn't act fast enough to clean up that oil spill last week. Nothing. Last night was boring and pointless. So is today."

"We've got bubkes," Xander added.

Anya, a former demon herself, and Xander's girlfriend, glanced at him uncertainly. "Bubkes?"

"Nada," Xander told her. "Zilch. Zip. Zero. Squat. Diddly." He shrugged. "Bubkes."

"Odd," Anya told him. She shook her head ever so slightly, an expression of frustration with the confusing world around her that was almost as common as the disparaging tone she took with most everyone. "It sounds almost like a sexual act."

"Oh, for God's sake," Giles muttered under his breath. The two of them did go on a bit about the more carnal aspects of their relationship.

"You're right," Xander said thoughtfully. "I think it's our job to invent that. Bubkes. We'll be the first."

"Do you two mind?" Giles snapped. "What we're dealing with here is quite serious. An infestation of new vampires led by an ancient demon-god. Lucy Hanover visits Buffy in a dream to warn her that something terrible is on the horizon just as she runs across this new group? I'm certain there's a connection. I suggest you get serious about working with me to figure out where these new arrivals are secreting themselves, or simply take your . . . distractions with you and go elsewhere."

Anya grinned, an amiable expression on her face. "Excellent," she said, climbing to her feet. "Let's go, Xander. We've only made it halfway through the *Kamasutra* and there are dozens of—"

Xander had the good sense to be somewhat embarrassed. "Um, Anya? That was sarcasm. Hard to tell with Giles, I know. But he needs help and was kidding about wanting us to leave." Then Xander frowned and glanced at Giles. "Right?"

"Not terribly certain of that myself," Giles replied dryly. "But, yes, I could use all the help I can get. I don't know why Buffy and Willow have not yet called me back."

"The Buffster's got nothing or she would have called you this morning, don't you think?" Xander said. "She went down to Willy's Alibi Room, intimidated Willy. If she'd gotten anything from him she would have called."

Giles glanced across the room at his phone, then glared down at the map on the table as if it were purposely withholding information from him. In a way, he almost felt as though it were.

"I suppose," he allowed. "And if anything had happened to her, Willow would have informed us this morning."

"Or she might have, if she wasn't so ticked off at Buffy," Anya interjected.

Both Xander and Giles looked at her with identical expressions of confusion.

Anya only rolled her eyes. *"Men.* You never pay attention. I'd bet someone's soul—not my own, of course—that Willow stayed at Oz's last night and hasn't spoken to Buffy at all today."

"Right," Giles snapped. He pushed back his chair and gathered the map up in his hands. "Let's head over there straightaway. If this Camazotz identified her as the Slayer, it's quite possible that—"

The phone rang.

Giles hurried to pick it up. "Keep looking," he told Xander and Anya. He interrupted the second ring.

"Hello?"

"Hey, it's me," Buffy said. "Sorry I haven't gotten back to you yet. I had classes and then library time."

"Yes, well, I admire your dedication to your classwork, Buffy, but Lucy Hanover's warning was a bit ominous, wouldn't you say? This situation with Camazotz requires our full focus."

"I'm on it," she said coldly. "I will save the world, as usual, all right? But there's also this thing called college that I have to do. Look, I know by now I'm not getting this paper done before Monday, so I won't hit any more classes today. But give me some breathing room, Giles. I wasn't the one with my girlfriend in town."

Startled as he was by her obvious anger and frustration, Giles hesitated. He wanted to defend himself, to argue that he had not shirked his duties at all while Olivia had been visiting, and in fact it had soured their visit somewhat. But he worried that, stressed as she was, Buffy might see that as an accusation.

"Are you all right?" he asked, as gently as he could.

"Peachy," she replied, but her voice was cold.

"Funny, you don't sound at all peachy. Buffy, one of the first lessons taught to any Slayer is that in order to survive you must learn to adapt, to improvise, to react to any situation fluidly and quickly. In your admirable attempt to create an orderly life for yourself, I fear you may have forgotten that."

"That's what I'm doing, Giles. Reacting. So I'm trying to create order out of the chaos that's been my life since the day I found out I was the Slayer. Is that wrong?"

He sighed. "You live your life in chaos, I'm afraid. In order to combat it, you immerse yourself in it. It's one of the sacrifices you make in exchange for the gifts of the Slayer, the power to keep the rest of the world safe from that very same chaos."

There was a long pause before Buffy spoke again. "I don't know if I can live like that anymore. If I give up trying to make sense out of things . . ."

"Buffy, you know you have my full support in that effort. It's simply that there are times—"

"I know," she replied sadly. "It's fine. I'll work it out. Moving on, now. I left my hand print on Willy's throat last night, but he's got nothing. Heard about the bat-faced vamps, but no word on who they are, why they're here, and where they're hanging their hats."

"Bubkes," Giles muttered.

On the other end of the line, Buffy paused. "You've

been watching old reruns of *Hill Street Blues* again, haven't you?"

"You were moving on?" he reminded her.

"I did a short patrol downtown, cemetery sweep, went by the Bronze. Fashion crimes notwithstanding, not a peep from anything soulless. Did a run through Docktown. Lot of tattoos, none of them bats."

As Giles listened to Buffy rattle off her actions of the night before, he stared at the map on the table and mentally traced the path of her patrol. It ended at Docktown, the section of Sunnydale used as a shipping port for a century. The Fish Tank, where she'd first run into the minions of Camazotz, was on the north side of Docktown, closest to the wharfs where vessels would be moored. The Kat Skratch Club was farther south and another block or two inland.

Both were far from the center of town, which was usually teeming with young life, and almost always ended up the primary target of vampires in Sunnydale. It was also much closer to the Hellmouth, which he believed drew them with almost magnetic power. Supernatural creatures in town did not generally stray far beyond its influence.

Docktown. And to the west, nothing but Pacific Ocean.

"Buffy," Giles said, his voice laden with regret. "I'm an absolute fool."

"You tell me this now, after I've been taking your advice all this time?"

"It's got to be a ship," he said. "The new House of

Bats, the lair of Camazotz." Giles glanced up at Xander and Anya, who had risen from the floor to come stand by the table and study the map with him. "It has to be a ship. Somehow they managed not to attract undue attention from customs and the harbormaster, even though they all have that brand on their faces."

"Makes sense," Xander admitted. "But they've got to have someone with a human face doing their nasty bidding. You can't make a whole ship invisible. There's gotta be a record of it somewhere."

On the phone, Buffy echoed his words. "That would explain why I haven't seen any of them in town. Yet. And even if you're wrong, we're no worse off than we have been. But how do we pinpoint them exactly? Breaking into every ship moored off Sunnydale is gonna be risky from the getting-arrested perspective, and really time-consuming."

"It might be possible to find what we need through a computer search. Otherwise, I think I may have an idea for a magickal solution. Either way, you should call Willow."

"Why don't I go down and talk to the harbormaster?" Buffy offered.

"You could try that," Giles admitted. "But he'd have no real reason to cooperate, and it would be inadvisable to try to intimidate anyone connected to the local authorities. We need to be prepared to search for them electronically, and mystically. For that, we need Willow."

* * *

After Buffy hung up the phone, she stared at it for almost a full minute without moving. Giles wanted her to call Willow. There was no question in Buffy's mind that Willow *could* help, but she disagreed with Giles that it was necessary. Even if it meant a little intimidation of the harbormaster, or the ship-to-ship search she knew she didn't have time for, Buffy thought those would be better. Or, at least, a part of her did. The other part recognized that Willow and Giles were probably right. But she feared that possibility. If that were true, a little voice whispered in the back of her mind, then the day might come when she would have to choose between her life as Buffy Summers, and her obligations as the Slayer.

Making that choice would tear her apart.

Buffy wished that she had been more insistent with Giles, that she had told him that they should all just stay there and continue their research. Instead, she knew, she would have to do her best to keep them all safe, yet another responsibility on her shoulders. But she would handle it.

She would.

Reluctantly, she dialed Oz's number.

He picked up on the third ring. "Hey."

"It's Buffy. Is Willow around?"

"She went to pick up pizza."

A surprisingly powerful wave of relief swept through Buffy. Giles thought they needed Willow. Having her around would certainly make things easier. But being the Slayer wasn't about making things easy.

If Willow wasn't around, maybe she would be able to send Giles home—tell him they would just try in the morning.

Then she could look into it herself, in her own way. The hard way.

"Buffy? Something going on?" Oz asked.

"Could you ask her to do something for me?" she began. Then she explained to him about the computer search, the little bit of illegal hacking that Giles wanted her to do. It couldn't hurt to have her do that, at least. Sitting at the keyboard was safe.

"I'll try to call later, see if she's got anything."

"I'll let her know," Oz replied. "She'll be glad."

His words carried more meaning, as always, but Buffy did not ask him to elaborate.

Darkness had fallen by the time Buffy made it to Docktown. When she reached The Fish Tank she stood in the shadows of a crumbling apartment house a block or so away and scanned the street. Across from the sleazy bar, she spotted Giles's ancient Citroën parked and dormant. Without the engine running, the thing looked almost abandoned. Though around here it wouldn't have been abandoned for long without being stripped.

Buffy knew better.

As she approached the car she passed a narrow alley where a homeless man had built a lean-to against a brick wall out of weathered wood he'd probably torn off the poorly kept docks just down the street, or picked up from the rocky shore beneath them. He noticed her noticing him, and then hissed at something in the shadows behind him. A chill ran through Buffy as she wondered whether he communicated with a creature of real darkness, or something from his fevered imagination. She found that the latter possibility unnerved her more.

Though she continued to move mostly in the shadows of buildings, Buffy picked up her pace. A moment later she stood behind the Citroën. Inside, in the dim light thrown from the guttering neon of The Fish Tank across the street, she could see Giles behind the wheel. He had a greasy brown paper sack of fried clams, French fries, and a can of soda. Not his usual cuisine, but she figured he had to pick something up in a rush. She couldn't blame him. It took her a moment to realize she'd eaten nothing since breakfast, but even now she did not feel like eating. Her stomach felt small and tight as a fist, like it couldn't have fit a single bite.

Later, when it was over. Then she would eat.

Buffy crouched down beside the car and rapped on Giles's window. He started, dropped a fried clam, then cursed about the tartar sauce he'd gotten on his sweater.

He motioned for her to come around the other side. Buffy slid into the passenger seat beside him while Giles tried to clean off his sweater. When he looked up, he was clearly mystified.

"You're by yourself? What happened to Willow?"

Buffy stiffened slightly. "I called Oz's, but she was out. I explained to him about the computer search, but I'm thinking we're going to have to postpone the magick until morning."

"Did you impress upon Oz the urgency of our situation?"

She shrugged. "Willow wasn't around, Giles. Oz isn't a witch. I guess we can call and see if she's come back, now, but is another twelve hours going to make that much difference? If she does her Internet magic, we may not even need the witchy stuff."

Buffy raised an eyebrow as she regarded him.

Giles cleared his throat and shot her a withering glance. "Twelve hours could make an enormous difference, Buffy. Another night could cost any number of lives."

Buffy glanced out the window at the dingy street. "I'll stick around, patrol all night if I have to. As you know, tomorrow's Saturday. So I'll sleep in. Maybe I'll even do some sleuthing in Docktown, come up with something. You guys can keep researching the burning eyes thing, right?"

"Xander and Anya are doing precisely that. I've begun to believe this isn't a separate, undiscovered breed of vampire, merely vampires who have somehow been enhanced by Camazotz. They are following that line of research. However, regrettable as Willow's absence is, we should exhaust all avenues presently available to us in our efforts to locate their lair."

Giles started up the car and put it in gear.

"Hey!" Buffy said, startled. "Look, Giles, I'm serious. You can be of more help with the books. When it comes to patrolling, maybe handing out some bloody noses to get the information we need, that's Slayer business, right? I'll start with the harbormaster and go from there. Xander and Anya are probably canoodling back at your place. We're not going to figure out what we're up against with them hitting the books. I stay, make with the fisticuffs. It's what I do. You go, make with the cross-referencicuffs. It's what *you* do."

Giles shot her a brief, sidelong glance, one eyebrow arched curiously. "Buffy, I have been on patrol with you dozens, perhaps hundreds of times. Why are you so insistent upon excluding me? After all this time you cannot possibly be worried about my safety."

"I'm not," Buffy said dismissively.

"Well, that's a comfort, I suppose."

Buffy glanced away, then up at him again. "I'm worried about mine. You've told me yourself, Giles, that traditionally Slayers operated alone. They didn't have friends around like I do, people they could rely on. They also didn't have lives outside being a Slayer. Well, I do, or at least I'm trying to. If I'm going to lead two lives, I've got to work twice as hard at both. For the Slayer, that means I take the responsibility of being the Chosen One, of my duties, on myself. I was Chosen, no one else. Sometimes it sucks, but I have to learn not to rely on anyone else but me. One girl in all the world, remember? That's what you told me when we first met. Not 'one girl in all the world and her Watcher and her best friends and their boyfriends and girlfriends and whoever else we happen to pick up along the way.'

"It's on me, Giles. You go. I stay."

"Everyone needs help sometimes, Buffy. That's why Slayers have Watchers in the first place," Giles argued, gazing at her with obvious concern.

"But The Powers That Be don't choose Watchers. Just Slayers."

Giles removed his glasses and let them dangle from his fingers as he considered her words. At length he looked over at her again.

"Now is probably not the time to argue the point, Buffy. But have you forgotten what I said about threatening the harbormaster? I tend to think that, particularly if he's not involved, the local authorities might be a bit agitated. We'll drive over there, and I'll speak to him first. If he seems suspicious, then perhaps you can have a go at him."

Buffy started to argue, but Giles was obviously determined. She also had to admit to herself that it would be better if he approached the harbormaster first. Not that she was happy about it. But there was little she could do except go along with him.

For the moment.

There was still a light burning in the harbormaster's office. Buffy had argued the point again, but Giles had insisted she wait in the car. Contrary to what she was trying to prove, Buffy could not do everything. Case in point, he was certain that the harbormaster would be much more likely to have a conversation about his work with an adult than a teenage girl.

He parked the Citroën a block and a half away and walked down to the office. It was a small building, not more than two or three rooms, overlooking the ocean, appropriately enough. The hours were posted on the door and it was long past official closing time, but Giles took the light on inside as a good sign.

There was no bell, so he rapped lightly on the door. Just when he would have rapped again, the doorknob rattled and then the big oak door was hauled open.

"What the hell do you want?" growled a bearded, gray-haired man with a cigar jutting from between his clenched jaws.

Giles stared at him. The man was almost a caricature of what he imagined a harbormaster ought to look like. He tore his eyes away, though. The last thing he wanted was to offend the man with such improprieties.

"You're the harbormaster, I take it?"

"Do you see the time?" the man demanded.

"Indeed I did, sir. But if I might have a moment. I'm an . . . investigative journalist and I had a few questions about recent goings-on here in Docktown. Gang presence, to be precise."

The harbormaster narrowed his eyes and puffed on his cigar, regarding Giles with great suspicion and likely more than a touch of xenophobia.

"You're British," the man said.

"Yes."

"What the hell does a Brit want with poking around Docktown asking questions? What business is it of yours what goes on down here?"

Giles hesitated. He had been afraid that this would not work, but it was not as if the man would have believed him a police officer, or answered questions if he had told the truth.

"As I said, sir, I'm an investigative journalist working for the *L. A. Times* and I'm looking into recent gang activity here," he insisted. With nothing to lose, he pressed on. "Apparently there has been a spate of violence by a group of ruffians with a very distinguishing mark. They all have a bat tattooed on their faces."

"Hrrrm," the old man grunted. He scratched his beard and puffed on his cigar. Then he let out a blast of smoke that swirled around Giles's face and nearly made him retch. "What'd you say your name was?"

"Robert Travers."

After another moment's thought, the harbormaster rolled the cigar around between his teeth and then nodded. "Might be I've heard something about that. Might be one of the dock rats I know's even seen something. You payin' for information?"

Giles smiled. "Of course."

The old man's eyes narrowed. "You just stay right there while I make a call."

"Absolutely. I'm at your service."

The old man closed the door.

Gulls cawed overhead in the darkness. The sky was a bit overcast, with very few visible stars. A car horn beeped far off and it drew Giles's attention to the road. So few cars down here this time of night, though he could hear a truck rumbling nearby. Metal clanked as the rise and fall of the ocean rocked the floating docks just down from the harbormaster's office.

Time went by.

Eventually, with a frown, he glanced at his watch and pressed the button to illuminate it. Nine-seventeen. He hadn't checked the time before, but he had the impression it had been at least five minutes, perhaps closer to ten, that he'd been left standing out here on the stoop. He wondered if the old man had simply been pulling his leg, making a fool of him.

Giles stepped away from the door and glanced up the street at his car. It was dark inside, though, and he could not see Buffy. With a sigh he went back to his post and tapped his foot as he waited.

At nine twenty-two, he rapped on the door again, more loudly than the first time.

It took longer for the harbormaster to open the door this time. When he did, he wore a cruel smile.

"You're a persistent one, ain'tcha?" the old man grumbled.

"It's my job," Giles replied.

"You do yours," the harbormaster said, chewing his cigar and hitching up his ragged blue jeans, "and I'll do mine."

With that, his hands flashed out with inhuman quickness and latched around Giles's throat. The old man spat out his cigar as he hauled Giles inside the office and tossed him across the room.

Giles crashed into the harbormaster's desk, shouting as his back struck its edge, then went down on the dirty wooden floor.

The harbormaster hissed at him. Even under the scraggly gray beard, Giles could see the fangs.

CHAPTER 6

This is taking too long, Buffy thought. She leaned over the dashboard and peered through the windshield.

Giles stood just outside the door to the harbormaster's office. As Buffy studied him, he glanced at his watch. *So I'm not the only one who thinks this is taking too long,* she thought.

A moment later Oz's van pulled up behind her. Buffy grimaced. This was complicating things even further, and she did not want that. With a glance up at the harbormaster's office to check on Giles and to make sure no one was looking out the window, Buffy climbed out of the car and went back to the van.

Willow was in the passenger seat. Buffy was simultaneously annoyed and pleased with her arrival.

Above and beyond the call of duty. The window was down.

"Hey," Willow began.

Buffy shushed her. "Open the back."

The back door popped open and Buffy went around and climbed in, only to find herself face to face with Xander.

"Hey," he said. "What's Giles doing, just standing there?"

Buffy narrowed her gaze, worried. "I don't know, exactly. Waiting for the harbormaster. The guy came to the door once, then shut it, and now Giles is just waiting. What are you guys doing here, anyway?"

Oz kept his eyes on Giles, but Willow turned around in her seat to face Buffy and Xander in the back.

"We thought we should back you up," Willow said. "When Oz told me you called, I tried calling back. Obviously you're not there, so I called Giles's. Xander told me what was going on. We picked him up and came here. Just in case. Figured Anya could handle the research for a little while."

"Thanks." Buffy smiled. "But we've got it covered, I think. You guys should get back. Research. Pizza. No worries."

"Already ate the pizza," Willow explained. "Or Xander did."

"Hey!" Xander protested. "Research makes me hungry."

"What doesn't?" Buffy asked.

"You didn't mention a spell," Willow said.

Buffy looked at her. "What?"

"When you talked to Oz. You didn't mention anything about a spell but Xander said Giles wanted me to get some stuff, do a locator spell or something. I could have gotten the ingredients together."

"You weren't around, Will. I thought we could just do the spell tomorrow. Besides, Giles wanted to talk to the harbormaster, see if he knows anything," Buffy replied.

There was a sort of tension in the van, but Buffy pretended not to notice and hoped Willow would just let it go. As if the conversation were over, she leaned forward slightly and looked past Willow through the windshield, to see that Giles still stood impatiently at the front door of the office.

"You think something's up?" Xander asked.

Buffy thought about that, let it roll around in her mind a little. This part of Docktown was deserted late at night. Just a short walk would take them to The Fish Tank, where there would at least be a few people stumbling in or out of the place. But down here . . . nothing. Too much of nothing, in fact.

Through Willow's open window, she heard a siren wail somewhere far off. Out on the sea, the bell of a buoy tolled on and on as if it were forever midnight.

Buffy studied the doors and windows of the buildings around them. In several, the silver gray flickering of television sets cast eerie shadows. Most were dark, though. A horrible, queasy feeling roiled in her belly and the fine, downy hairs on her arms and the back of her neck prickled as though an electrical storm were about to sweep down upon them. Her heart beat a little faster.

"This isn't right," she said.

Willow and Xander also seemed spooked. They were staring out from the van as though at any moment the shadows themselves might come alive.

"You feel it too?" she asked.

Xander shrugged. "I don't know. I always feel a little bit like this when we're on monster duty."

But Willow met Buffy's gaze directly. "Something. You're right. I don't know exactly what it is, but . . . something."

"So you've got spider-sense, too?" Xander asked her.

"There's nothing supernatural about it," Willow told him. "Maybe we're all just paranoid. It is a bit freaky down here. But I'm with Buffy."

"I never should have let him go up there. Look, you should all go home," Buffy said as she rifled through her bag, pulled out the crossbow and handed it to Xander. "You're riding shotgun. I just want to be prepared if anything—"

"Buffy!" Xander interrupted. He pointed past her head, out the windshield.

The Slayer turned around just in time to see the old man haul Giles inside the harbormaster's office with inhuman strength. The door crashed shut behind them.

"Back me up, but don't get out of the van unless I tell you to."

As she leaped out of the van, Buffy's heart felt like stone in her chest. A feeling of profound dread, bone-deep, welled up within her. Though she sprinted down the street toward the harbormaster's office, it felt to her as though the world had slowed around her, as though the small shack was miles, rather than feet, away.

"Giles," she muttered under her breath, her friends almost completely forgotten in the car behind her. She heard the engine rattle to life and knew they would be following her in a moment.

But Giles might not have a moment.

Her legs pumped, the soles of her shoes slapped the cracked pavement, and her face felt suddenly cold, despite the exertion. The rest of the world disappeared and the only sound Buffy could hear was her own breathing. Everything else was muffled, as though she were underwater.

Buffy sprinted up to the door of the harbormaster's office, whipped a stake out from its sheath, and kicked the door in with such force that the frame splintered and was torn off its hinges. The place was trashed. Paperwork was strewn about the huge oak desk in the far corner. A lamp lay broken on the floor next to a phone that was off the hook. Both had been knocked off the desk. An old framed painting of a schooner about to crash onto the shore by a light-house hung nearly sideways on its hook. A shelf of books had been knocked over. Two other lights still burned in the room, dim, but plenty of illumination to allow Buffy to see the horror that was unfolding before her.

In a narrow doorway that led into another part of the office, Giles lay half in one room and half in the other. His pants leg was torn and blood had begun to seep through the cloth. He tried to sit up, eyes glazed over as he shook his head, blinking rapidly. His face was already bruised and cut, blood dripping down his chin from some unknown wound inside his mouth.

The vampire was hunched over him. In his sharp-clawed fist he held Giles by the front of his shirt. With his other hand, the gray-bearded vampire gripped Giles's throat. When Buffy crashed through the door, the vampire looked up at her and snarled. His appearance was startling to her. Rarely did she see vampires who looked *old*. Existing vampires usually bred only with the strongest and most attractive humans, which was why most of them looked so young and vibrant. Then it clicked in her mind; Camazotz's followers had made this man a vampire because he was the harbormaster. With his aid, their entry into the U.S. would be that much simpler.

The harbormaster hissed at her, bared his fangs. His brow was ridged and hideous, his eyes alive and feral, yet not burning like the others. Another mystery.

"Let him go," Buffy demanded.

The vampire laughed, a deep, throaty, gurgling sound. "Or what? You'll kill me? And if I free him, what then? You'll let me go? We're not all that stupid, you know."

With a grunt, the creature hauled Giles up and spun him around, holding him as hostage, as shield.

"Buffy . . . you must . . . go." Giles croaked.

The vampire rammed his head forward into the back of Giles's skull. The impact was loud, and sounded perilously fragile, as though something had broken. Buffy cringed and felt as though she might throw up. Giles's eyes rolled up to white and he went limp in the vampire's powerful hands.

Fury kindled within her like a furnace. She gripped the stake in her right hand even more tightly.

"Maybe you don't know who you're dealing with, moron," she snapped. "Or maybe you're just too stupid to know better. I'm Buffy Summers. I'm—"

"The Slayer."

The voice came from behind her. Buffy spun, put her back to the wall so that she could see both the doorway and the harbormaster. Amidst the shattered remains of the door stood a creature whose appearance made her breath catch in her throat. Naked from the waist up, the tall, hideous thing was hunched over and a pair of skeletal wings jutted up from his back. They looked as though they had been torn apart, or ravaged by fire. On his chest was an enormous scar, and at the center of the scar an open wound that seemed partially healed, as though it might never close completely.

His hair was black and thickly matted, as was his long beard. He had a short, ugly snout with wet slits for nostrils, and his chalky, green-white skin was pockmarked all over. Upon his forehead were ridges that resembled those of a vampire. From his mouth jutted rows of teeth like icicles, and his fingers were inhumanly long and thin, white enough to have been little more than bones.

But what struck her most deeply were his eyes. Blazing orange fire, just like its vampire followers.

"Camazotz," Buffy whispered, hating herself immediately for the horror and awe she heard in her own voice.

"I'm touched you know me."

The monster grinned.

"No wonder you live in a cave," Buffy sniffed dismissively. "Who'd go out, looking like that?"

Out of the corner of her eye she watched the harbormaster, just in case her taunting of the vampire's master would cause him to do something rash—like snap her mentor's neck. But the creature remained impassive. For his part, where many others would have raged at the insult, Camazotz merely grunted with amusement.

"The man means something to you," the demongod said. "Your Watcher?"

His voice was wet and thick, something trapped in quicksand and desperate to be free. There was an accent there as well, but nothing Buffy recognized, much like that of the bat-faces she had fought before.

Her gaze ticked toward Giles, still unconscious, and back to Camazotz. There was no percentage in lying. He was obviously far from stupid. But that didn't mean she had to tell the freak her life story.

"Not my Watcher. A friend," she admitted. She

hefted the stake in her right hand, turned its point toward him. "So you're the god of bats, huh? Considering the job description, those are pretty pitiful wings."

Camazotz actually flinched. While he had not responded at all to Buffy's previous taunt, this seemed to have gotten under his skin. Curious, Buffy gazed at him again, took in the bony things that jutted up from his hunchback.

"Sore spot, huh?" She gestured with the stake at his back. "Someone gave you a good mangling. Can you even fly with those?"

Camazotz lost all of the cool reserve he'd shown, and a primitive snarl split his features. His eyes flared and sparked.

"I knew I would have to destroy you to reach the Hellmouth, cow. I am prepared. My Kakchiquels are bred and raised by me. They do not fear you, girl, because they have never *heard* of you. They will face you without hesitation, down to the last of them, because they do not know what a Slayer is."

"They will," she promised, returning his snarl as she relaxed and tightened the grip on her stake. "I've killed bigger and badder and uglier than you. You want me? Come and get me." She stared at him, letting the moment of silence charge the air between them with crackling energy. Then she smiled.

"Let's get it on, stumpy."

The flesh of the ancient creature seemed almost to ripple with his rage. He shuddered, nostrils flaring, long needle teeth bared, and he rose up to his full height, about to lunge at her.

Then Camazotz smiled.

Buffy swore silently, her hopes dashed, her heart aching.

"You want to antagonize me into direct combat, believing you can destroy me and still save your . . . friend," Camazotz said, slippery voice tinged with wonder. "And maybe you would at that, Slayer. Maybe you would. But I have walked upon this Earth since before the human virus infected it, and I have grown cautious in that time."

Camazotz gestured to the harbormaster. "If she does not obey me instantly, kill him. *Drink* him."

Tongue flicking out over his teeth, Camazotz glared at her. All trace of humor was gone from his horrid countenance. "Throw the stake down. On your knees and crawl to me."

Her heart raced and Buffy tried not to let Camazotz see the effect of his words. For all her bluster, she knew he had her. But her mind raced along all the possible avenues of the stalemate in an instant, and she knew there was only one possible choice. If she did as he commanded, they were both dead. If she attacked, Giles would be savaged, possibly murdered, before she could reach him. She had to bank on Camazotz's keeping Giles alive to use as a lure to try to destroy her.

One choice. He might still die, but it's my only choice.

With a final glance at Giles and a burning in her
eyes that might have been tears if she dared allow
herself to feel the pain in her heart, Buffy turned
away from both of them and ran at the harbormaster's
desk. Camazotz screamed behind her, but Buffy did
not slow. She leaped up onto the desk and dropped
her shoulder as she crashed through the window and
onto the street beyond, around the side of the building from the main road. She hit the pavement in a
shower of shattered glass, sharp edges slicing her
skin.

Hating herself, filled with fear for Giles, she rolled
and then jumped to her feet. It had been her only
choice. Now she had to get to Willow and the guys
and get—

Buffy rounded the front of the building and froze,
mouth open in horror. The Kakchiquels were there, arrayed in the street like an army. Perhaps two dozen,
maybe even more, and each of them wore Camazotz's
brand tattooed across his face. Or her face. Lots of hers.

But they did not even notice Buffy. Their attention
was on the van.

Oz's van was parked in the midst of this sea of
monsters, this swarm of silent vampires. Through the
windshield, Buffy could see Oz and Willow, frozen
as though they were afraid that any motion would set
off the vampires. They dared not attack as long as
they were not attacked, so pitiful were the odds.

Then the Kakchiquels began their chant. It rose in
volume but lowered in pitch, until it shook the ground

beneath her feet and thundered against her like the distant thump of fireworks on the Fourth of July.

It was a moment. A single moment.

Camazotz emerged from the harbormaster's office, blazing orange eyes upon her. The demon-god dragged Giles along by the throat as though he were a rag doll. For a moment, Buffy worried that he was already dead. His glasses were long gone and the blood on his face had begun to dry. His eyes were glazed and dull. A corpse. That's what came into her mind. He was a corpse.

But he still breathed.

That was enough to break her paralysis, to splinter the frozen moment like a thin layer of ice across a pond.

"Oz!" she screamed. "Drive!"

Camazotz screamed something in a language Buffy did not recognize. It was as though a switch had been thrown, for the Kakchiquels surged to horrible, vicious life. They shattered the windshield of the van before Oz could even put it in gear. A startlingly tall female with rings piercing her face in painful adornment used both fists to smash the passenger window just as the van's engine roared and it shot forward a few yards, battering four vampires back and off their feet, and crushing one beneath the tires. The broken leech shrieked his pain, but he would not die. Could not die. It would be in agony for ages.

Good, Buffy thought.

She waded into the swarm with no grace or elegance at all. *Odds like this,* she thought, *it's all or nothing.* Vampires were all around her, clustering like insects as they tried to find an opening in her defenses. Buffy cracked a backhand across the bridge of a nose, snapped a high kick off that shattered a ribcage, stamped hard enough to break a leg . . . too many to focus on killing them. She had to cripple them instead.

But after the first few seconds, a rhythm did work its way into her bones, into her muscles. As if it were merely a closed-fisted blow, she punched the stake through one heart, then a second, parried a fist, dodged a kick, then dusted a third. Ash and cinder blew in a cloud around her, stealing the salt smell of the ocean from the air and replacing it with the smell of moldering tombs and unfiltered cigarettes.

Someone shouted, grunted, barked a war cry, and she knew it was her own voice. Sweat ran down her face and she knew she had descended inside herself, to a place where only the warrior remained. In the heat of battle, Buffy went away, leaving only the hunter. The Slayer.

Bat-faces lunged at her but she didn't even see them anymore. All she saw was that spot on their chests where the stake should go, and the tender places on their bodies she could break.

Then, lost in that place of blood and perfect fury, she heard her name tear the night, slicing through her battle fever. Buffy glanced up at the sound and saw the same bat-face woman, tall as an Amazon, pierced all over, dragging Willow out through the windshield even as Oz tried to gun the engine and run her over. But half a dozen Kakchiquels had lifted the rear of the van so it could not move. The rear window shattered, and Xander popped the crossbow out the window, shot one through the heart. He dusted, but another was there to take his place instantly.

"Damn it, no!" Buffy screamed.

With a leap, she spun and kicked the bat-face in front of her hard enough to break his neck. Buffy landed and ran for the van. Vampires blocked her way but she leaped up and over them and onto the roof just in time to stake the vampire who was trying to drag Willow out of the van. She exploded in a cloud of dust and Willow dropped back through the windshield, bleeding from several long scrapes on her arms and belly.

"Get out of here!" Buffy snapped as she leaped down to the pavement.

Through the shattered windshield, she could see Xander notching another crossbow bolt in the back of the van. Oz watched Willow expectantly, revving the engine. Willow stared at Buffy.

"But Giles—" Willow began.

"We can't help him if we're dead," Buffy interrupted. Then she leaped up on top of the van again, jumped off the back and drop-kicked two of the vamps holding up the car. She dusted a third.

"Now!" she cried, turning back to see Xander firing another bolt from the crossbow through the back window.

Oz floored it. Willow stared at Buffy through the open rear window, face etched with despair. More vampires grabbed onto the van as it went, but Oz ran over several of them and in seconds was dragging two down the street.

As Buffy fought, she tried to watch as they made their way to safety. They were almost out of sight, away from the Kakchiquels, but one final leech still clung to the roof of the van. As Buffy glanced over again, Xander stuck his upper body through the broken rear window. The vampire rose up, about to lunge at him, and Xander fired a bolt into his chest.

Dusted.

The van rolled out of sight.

Safe, Buffy thought. *Now Giles.*

She turned to seek out Camazotz and her unconscious former Watcher. At least a dozen Kakchiquels were dead by her count, but there seemed so many more. Slayer or not, Buffy was growing tired. A spinning kick, a hard elbow, a thrust of the stake and for just a moment her path was clear. Camazotz still stood in front of the harbormaster's office. Buffy stared at him.

Their eyes met.

Gazes locked together, their contact was intimate with the knowledge that Buffy could not win.

Camazotz lifted Giles up with one hand. The man's head lolled to the side but his eyes were open and it looked as though he might be waking, finally. Then the ancient demon, the god of bats, drew one long talon along Giles's throat and blood began to flow.

Amongst the surviving vampires arrayed near their master, two came forward. Clownface and Bulldog.

"Giles, no!" Buffy cried, frozen, paralyzed by the flicker of fire in Camazotz's eyes, and the inescapable truth that she had lost.

Then she screamed his name again and rushed toward the vampires. Camazotz began to laugh.

As if awakened by her cries, Giles began to fight back. He roared his outrage as he gazed around at the vampires surrounding him, filling the street. Buffy tried desperately to reach him, staked one vampire, kicked another in the jaw so hard it nearly tore his head off. Then, through the crush of Camazotz's minions, Giles saw Buffy, and his screaming stopped.

Their eyes met.

"Get out of here!" he snapped at her. "You can't defeat him alone. Get Angel. Get—"

"Shut him up!" Camazotz snapped.

Bulldog held Giles, and Clownface struck him with a single, hard blow to the skull. The Watcher was dazed and fell limp once more, and the two vampires handed him over to the others of their brood.

"Choose, Slayer," the god of bats instructed her.

Buffy wanted to scream her hatred at him, but the words would not come. Only anguish. She released it in a shriek that seemed to tear from her lungs and scrape her throat raw, and she ran at Camazotz.

There were vampires in between.

Off guard, driven only by her fear for Giles, Buffy did not see the baseball bat cutting through the air, nor did she hear it split the wind. It cracked against her head and the wooden bat broke in two as she went down hard on the pavement.

Blinking back the pain, brushing away the blood in her eyes, she looked up. The ghost-white vampire woman she thought of as Clownface stood above her, grinning like an idiot. A heartbeat later, Bulldog came up beside her.

Then they started kicking Buffy.

A rib broke, maybe two.

A foot hit her in the face and a tooth rattled loose. Her mouth was bleeding.

She rolled over and took a kick in the spine that shot pain to every nerve ending. Her eyes flashed open and she saw, thirty yards away, the end of the road. The docks thrust out from the land and the ocean beyond was black as the abyss.

Clownface swung a kick at her eyes. Buffy grabbed her ankle, twisted it enough to throw her off balance. Then she whipped her own feet around and dropped Bulldog's legs out from under him.

Two more came at her but they could not stop her. Buffy cut them down with a flurry of quick blows and ran on. The chanting had stopped during the brawl but it picked up again now and Camazotz roared something unintelligible. Buffy bit her lip and prayed to whatever powers were on her side that he would keep Giles alive as a hostage. For insurance.

Then, brutalized and bleeding, clutching her chest where her cracked ribs blazed with pain, she reached the dock, ran its length, and dove into the churning waves.

At least two vampires came after her. Underwater she heard the disturbance as they dove in.

And they don't need to breathe, she thought. Hope seemed to be seeping from her along with blood.

Buffy swam deeper, farther, kicking and pulling the water past her, moving into the murky depths of the Pacific and praying that they would not find her before morning.

Yet morning was so far away.

And she was running out of air.

She had drowned before, of course. But this time, there was no one around to bring her back. Her eyes were stung by the salt water but Buffy kept them open, peering into the blackness. Her lungs burned. The darkness in her eyes was not merely the shadows under water, but an encroaching dimming of vision.

Her limbs slowed.

Her mouth opened and she choked back her first gulp of sea water.

She stopped swimming.

"Buffy."

She squeezes her eyes shut, tight against the blazing heat that beats down upon her. Copper blood tangy in her mouth, she chokes on something and hacks and spits it out, rolling her face on the ground.

"Buffy."

Eyes snap open, wincing from the sun. Chest heav-

ing, throat ragged, too painful to speak, almost too agonizing to breathe.

"Buffy."

Moist sand beneath her bruised cheek and water washes up over her legs and lower torso. Eyes slitted, she peers up to see who speaks her name so urgently.

A ghost. And oh so appropriate, for she feels as though she must be dead. Lucy Hanover lingers in the air, a phantom through which she can see the trees swaying farther up the beach. A specter whose grim features speak of horrible things, whose eyes are like ghosts themselves, a ghost of a ghost, Lucy haunting herself with what she sees and what she knows.

She has no legs.

Instead, there is only a kind of mist, like the low fog that sometimes creeps across the ocean in the early morning. Perhaps that's what it is, after all.

She floats.

"Buffy."

"Lucy." Her own voice is little more than the rasp of a crab scuttling across sand.

"Catastrophe—"

"Is coming," Buffy chokes. "Kinda got it."

"No."

Lucy hovers closer, places her hands over Buffy's eyes. The heat of the sun that had seared them disappears, replaced by a soothing coolness that seeps through her body. Relaxing.

But . . .

"No?"

"Camazotz is not the threat I warned you of. At least, not entirely. The Prophet says there is more. A plague of vampirism is coming. A plague that will blot the sun from the sky above the Hellmouth."

"Not Camazotz?"

"Not entirely. I only communicate what little she has seen."

"My fault?"

Lucy weeps the ghosts of tears. "Yes. I'm sorry."

Buffy has no tears. "I don't care."

"What do you mean?"

"Giles," the Slayer says. "The only thing that matters. I left him."

Sad understanding illuminates Lucy's face. Blue sky and clouds behind her, through her. "You lived. Your other choice was death."

"Not dead?" Buffy feels the shock of it rushing through her, filling her up even as waves wash over her again.

"Not yet."

"Buffy?"

The dream shattered and blew away. Her eyes flickered open and she cringed from the harsh sun, tasted wet sand in her mouth and felt the damp squelch of it beneath her. The surf washed in, tiny waves almost touching her. The beach. She had made it to the beach.

A pair of familiar silhouettes made shadows across her body.

"Are you all right?"

It was Willow. Her eyes brimmed with tears. Oz stood beside her, his normally impassive face taut with concern.

"Will," Buffy rasped. The pain in her throat was excruciating. "I think I almost drowned," she whispered, and that didn't hurt quite as much. "I feel like hell."

"Looks like you've been there," Oz told her.

"God, Buffy, we've been out all morning looking for you. I thought you were dead."

So did I, Buffy thought.

Willow hugged her gently, careful not to touch anywhere that was bruised. Buffy's heart nearly broke, so grateful was she for the simple warmth of her best friend's touch, for the bond between them, and the strength that Willow gave her in that moment.

Then she remembered.

"Willow," Buffy said, stricken, almost unable to breathe. "They got Giles. Camazotz did. I don't know if he's still . . . I don't know . . ."

Lips pressed together, determined, hiding her own anxiety and grief, Willow nodded. "We'll find him. I swear we will."

CHAPTER 7

"I should've stayed."

Buffy felt numb all over, and cold. Though her cuts and bruises had begun to heal, even to fade, she felt completely drained, as though her life force had been siphoned away from her by her fight with Camazotz. And, in a way, it had.

Willow laid a hand upon hers and Buffy grasped her friend's fingers as though they were the only thing keeping her from drowning. Drowning. Though they sat, now, in the dormitory room they shared, Buffy felt as though she had never washed up on the sand, as though she still rolled beneath the waves with the ebb and flow of the tide.

Oz leaned against the back of the door. Anya sat on the edge of Willow's bed, with Xander stretched out on it behind her. Like Willow, he had scratched his whole body on the broken glass in the van. A line of black stitches was sewn tightly into the left side of his forehead. Apparently he had stitches on his back as well, but Buffy hadn't asked to see them.

Xander was unusually silent. And in pain.

"God, I can't believe this," Buffy muttered, and shook her head.

"Hey," Willow said softly. "You did the only thing you could do."

Eyes searching, Buffy gazed about the room at her friends, then out the window, and finally, at Willow. "Will . . . I *ran*. Giles could be dead. I *ran!*"

"No. You escaped with your life. Buffy, there's a difference. You said yourself that if you'd stayed you'd both be dead now. It was your only possible choice. Now we have a chance."

"If they haven't . . ." Buffy could not finish the thought.

Xander winced as he sat up to look at her. "They haven't," he said flatly. His eyes lacked their usual sparkle, but there was an intensity in them Buffy had never seen there before. A sharp edge, a glint of light as if off a finely honed blade. Pain and rage could do that. Buffy knew almost better than anyone.

"Xand . . ."

He cut her off with the wave of a hand. "It wasn't a trap, Buffy," he told her. "But it might as well have been. Camazotz knew you'd come looking, and he was ready. Giles poked around, got the vampy harbormaster suspicious enough to call his boss, the bat-god. He didn't kill Giles then, and he could've. Easy. Camazotz didn't kill him either. He's their insurance policy. You know that's true. Instinctively you knew it then, or you wouldn't have gone for that swim."

Still numb, Buffy glanced around at the others. Oz had a grim expression on his face, eyebrows knit together. Anya was watching her expectantly. Willow's eyes were filled with both love and sorrow, and she cradled her arms as though to hide her own injuries from Buffy. But it was Xander's bruised, scraped face that drew her gaze the most. He stared at her intently, saying nothing more for what seemed too long.

"Two more things, Buff," he added. "Then I'm going to pass out, if nobody minds. First, Willow, Oz, and I'd be dead if not for you. I feel like I've been hazed into the vampire fraternity, but that's better than being a corpse. Second thing, I think Giles is still alive. Nothing else makes sense. Now, not to be Mr. Pushy Guy or anything, but kinda thinking maybe we ought to get up a posse, go and get him out of there."

All the weight of it, the responsibility for what had gone before and whatever was to come, felt impossibly heavy on Buffy's shoulders. With their eyes upon her she gazed down at the floor. Her nostrils flared and her teeth ground together, and the numbness began to leave her. She realized, suddenly, that it had been her own doing, that numbness, a way to keep the despair and anger and her fear for Giles at bay.

For a time, she had been lost.

No more.

"Buffy?" Willow ventured.

She placed her hand over Willow's, nodded once and stood up. Grim-faced, she paced the room once, mind awhirl not only with the events of the previous night, but with the ominous dream words of Lucy Hanover, the dire predictions of some distant spectral Prophet. While washed up on the beach, half-drowned and barely conscious, she had been visited by Lucy again. The ghostly Slayer had told her that Camazotz was not the danger she had previously been warned about. That troubled Buffy almost more than anything else. With Giles's life hanging in the balance and a threat as significant as Camazotz in town, she could not afford to be blindsided by something else.

"This is because of me," she whispered. "I got so carried away with trying to handle everything on my own that I . . ."

Buffy closed her eyes. The numbness threatened to sweep through her again but she shook it off. "Willow," she said quickly. "You can prepare the same spell Giles wanted to use. Let's assume you can locate their ship. Anything you can do, magickally, to hide us from them when we invade their lair? A glamour, something to make us invisible to them, give us the element of surprise?"

Willow frowned, deep in thought. "I don't know. Giles might . . ." She looked up guiltily. "Let me do some research. Maybe a cloaking glamour. A spell like that's serious magick, but—"

"Don't try it if there's any danger. I can't afford anything happening to you. To any of you." Buffy glanced around at her friends. "Here's the plan. Anya, you're with Willow. Research and magick preparation right-hand girl. Centuries of demonic hijinks have to be worth something, right? Oz, you're with me. Weapons gathering and recon."

"Hello?" Xander said, waggling the fingers of his right hand from his prone position on Willow's bed. "What's my mission: impossible?"

"I need you here," Buffy told him. "You have to wait for Angel."

That got their attention. Willow and Anya spoke in unison.

"Angel?"

Buffy nodded gravely. "As soon as we're done here I'm going to call him, tell him what's going on. I don't know if he'll come—"

"He'll come," Willow said sadly. "You know he'll come."

"I hope you're right," Buffy replied. "We can use all the help we can get. I didn't want to have to . . . but with what Lucy Hanover told me, we don't even know what else might be out there."

She turned to Willow. "We need to find out. We need to know more. That means summoning Lucy and trying to get a direct line of communication with this mystery-ghost Prophet. See if we can get her to say something more specific than 'you're doomed.' "

* * *

For once it was sunny outside . . . just when a little gloom would have been appropriate. Inside Buffy and Willow's room, the shades were pulled down so that only the thinnest glimmer edge of sunlight streamed through on either side. White candles were placed in a rough circle around the room and the white-orange flames that flickered from each of them seemed to sway in a breeze that came from nowhere.

Buffy and Willow sat opposite each other in the wooden chairs from their desks, which they had dragged over between their beds. With Xander and Anya on one bed and Oz on the other, the five of them formed a rough circle. From previous experience, Buffy knew that what they had thrown together was a sloppy séance, or summoning, or whatever the official name for it was. But they did not have time to worry about the niceties of such things. No time at all.

"Clear your minds," Willow instructed.

Her voice seemed somehow different to Buffy, deeper, more confident. It was as though at times like this, the teenage shell that surrounded Willow was stripped away to reveal the triumphant woman she would become in time. The hesitation, the tacit apology, that so often lingered in her voice and mannerisms had disappeared entirely. Radiant with this power, head tilted back and eyes closed, Willow seemed to flow with the candlelight, then merge with the energy in the room. Buffy thought she had never been more beautiful.

Willow's eyes snapped open, fixed directly on Buffy. "I said clear your minds."

"Oh," Buffy said sheepishly. "Sorry."

Eyes now closed, Buffy took a long, deep breath, let it linger within her for a moment, and then let it out as though it were her very last. It was a cleansing, meditative technique Giles had taught her way back during sophomore year of high school. It worked.

Giles.

Buffy cleared her mind as best she could, but thoughts of Giles lingered like prisoners in the deepest dungeons of her mind.

"With hope and light and compassion, we open our hearts to all those walkers between worlds who might hear my plea and come to aid us in this dark hour," Willow began, intoning the words slowly.

Buffy felt Xander's hand grip hers on one side, and Oz's do the same on the other. It was as though the innate power within Willow, the peace and mystic qualities within her heart and soul that made her so naturally attuned to the energies of the supernatural, had created a kind of electrical charge that ran through them all. A circuit of benevolent magick, a beacon to the souls to whom Willow now spoke.

Does she hear them when she closes her eyes? Buffy wondered. *Can she see them in her mind?* They had never talked about it, and for some reason, Buffy doubted she would ever ask. It seemed somehow too intimate, like asking the details of a passionate romance.

"Spirits of the ether, bear my voice along the paths of the dead, whisper my message to every lost soul and wanderer," Willow continued, voice lowering in timbre, becoming not unlike a kind of chant. "I seek the counsel of Lucy Hanover, she who was once a Slayer. She who holds high the lantern to light your path on the journey between worlds."

Giles.

Buffy frowned to herself as a sliver of sadness pushed past the defenses she had erected in her mind. Giles was alive. She would not believe anything else. But she knew what his fate might be, had seen how badly he had been beaten, seen the harbormaster's fangs in his flesh, the blood that flowed when Camazotz slashed his neck.

Reluctantly, she recalled the last time they had called upon Lucy Hanover's aid, and what Giles had said. *I want to be on record as having opposed this. Calling on the spirits of the dead is a tricky business.*

Undoubtedly, he was right. It had once been his job to know such things. But the hard truth was that at the moment, they had no choice. Without him, there seemed no other way to discover what they were truly up against, and what part, if any, Camazotz was to play in it. More than that, what part Buffy herself was to play in the danger ahead.

After half a minute's silence, Willow spoke again, this time her voice barely rose above a whisper. "Lucy, do the lost ones bring my voice to you?"

The answer was immediate.

"They do."

Buffy opened her eyes. The others were all looking as well. Lucy Hanover was there in the center of the circle they had created. The flickering candles and the slices of sunlight that leaked around the shades made a dim gray illumination that washed out the room, washed out the ghost herself, so that she seemed less a thing of mist and spirit than an antique sepia photograph somehow projected onto the air.

"Greetings, friend Willow," Lucy said, her voice sounding hollow and distant. Then the ghost turned her dark eyes upon Buffy. "We meet again, Slayer. I am sorry for what has happened, Buffy. The ghost roads are ripe with gossip and dire news."

Ice spread across Buffy's heart. "Giles?" she asked, almost too afraid to speak his name. "He's not . . ."

Lucy's eyes were kind, then. "No. He is not yet among us. There is time for you, yet, to go to him."

Though she had felt almost suffocated by her concern for him, it was not until Buffy heard those words that she truly understood how afraid she had been. A tiny voice in the back of her mind had been taunting her all along with the thought that it was already too late, that he was dead.

Buffy nodded. "I'll get him back."

"Lucy," Willow interrupted, "Buffy has shared with us the things you told her in her dreams. About this Prophet. Your warnings have been so vague and with all that is happening, with Giles captured and the dangers we all face, we need to know all we can. There must be more to this prophecy."

Lucy shook her head sadly. Her image seemed to shudder, to flicker like the candlelight, and the swirl of mist that obscured her lower half extended, as though she had somehow stood taller.

"I am no seer, Willow. I cannot promise that what this Prophet has scried will come to pass, for I know her only by what the lost souls have whispered. They say that she can see the future, that the mists of time are clear for her. I have only informed the Slayer of her predictions so that you might all be wary."

Willow glanced over at Buffy with deep concern, seemingly at a loss for how to continue.

Buffy did not hesitate. "Can we talk to her?"

"If she will speak with you," Lucy replied in that hollow voice. "I will seek her."

Then, as if she had never been there at all, she was simply gone.

Oz was the first to break the circuit. He let go of Buffy's hand and then Buffy released her grip on Xander's, and they all exhaled loudly, blinking and looking at one another in silence.

Anya examined Xander as though she thought the exertion might have drained him. Buffy thought it was both sweet and creepy, like a coroner autopsying the corpse of a loved one. Willow seemed to have shrunk a bit, and she looked slightly lost as she glanced around the room, obviously uncertain what to do next.

Oz broke the silence. "Well," he said. "That was bracing."

"What now?" Xander gazed at Buffy, sort of nodding his head to prod her to answer the question. His eyebrows went up as further punctuation. "Buff?"

"We wait."

"How long do we wait?" Anya pressed. "I need to pee. Though some think it erotic, I have always found the process rather revolting and would rather it remain a private thing."

Buffy wondered if her facial expression was enough to convey her horror and disgust. "With you on the revolting . . . revulsion. Please. Be my guest."

Anya rose and strode toward the door.

A gust of wind nearly knocked her off her feet. It cut through the room fast and hard enough to scour the walls. In her rat cage, Amy squealed and ran in circles. The windows were closed tight, but the wind tugged at all of them. Impossibly, though the flames guttered with the gusts, the candles still burned.

Then, in a single moment, as though they were atop a birthday cake, every candle in the room was snuffed.

Somehow, even the slices of daylight that had filtered in around the shades were gone.

The wind swirled tighter and tighter until it no longer touched them, instead creating a miniature tornado in the center of the room. Then the wind itself seemed to bleed an oily black, the oil to spread and flow and take form. The wind slowed.

It *became* something.

"She has agreed to speak with you."

Buffy glanced quickly toward the window and saw the ghost of Lucy Hanover hovering there, watchful. Wary.

When she looked back, the wind had died and the flowing black core of it had coalesced into a figure, the silhouette of a woman. The Prophet had no face that Buffy could see, nor flesh, not even the diaphanous mist that gave Lucy shape. Instead, The Prophet was like a female-shaped hole in the center of the room, a black pit that lingered in the air like soot from a smokestack.

But it spoke. *She* spoke.

"Slayer. You summoned me. How may I be of service?"

Her voice was like the whisper of a lifelong smoker whose throat had been ravaged by cancer. Pained and ragged and knowing, in on the perversity of the joke.

Buffy spoke quickly. The sooner The Prophet was gone from the room, the happier she'd be.

"Lucy told me you'd seen something bad coming. Apocalypse-size evil, or at least the giant economy size. She also told me you thought it was going to be my fault. I need your help. Isn't there any way I can cut this thing off at the pass? Not make this mistake? And if there's no way to do that, then I need to know more about what this evil will be, what form it will take, and how I can combat it. There's a demon in town, an ancient, powerful—"

The Prophet laughed. Her obsidian form shimmered where it hung in the room, a wound between worlds. It was sickening to look at, though Buffy could not have said why.

"Not seeing the funny," Xander said abruptly.

Anya shushed him, and Buffy did not blame her. Dealing with beings like this, none of them should be inviting attention. But Buffy had no choice.

"You won't help, then?"

"Not won't. Cannot." The swirling shadow moved just the tiniest bit closer to Buffy then. *"The thing you fear has already been set in motion. The die is cast. Your mistake, Slayer, has already been made."*

"What?" Buffy asked, horrified. Her mouth dropped open. Her lungs refused to work. For a moment, even her heart seemed to refuse to beat. Then, shaking her head, she gasped a tiny, plaintive cry. "But I haven't done anything. How can that be? And nothing's changed."

"But it will," the Prophet told her. *"The future cannot be prevented now. Already the clockwork grinds on. But I can show you my vision, share with you the sight, so you may see what is coming and perhaps better prepare for it."*

Reeling, Buffy glanced at Willow and Oz, then at Xander and Anya. They all seemed as stricken by the specter's words as she was. By the window, Lucy Hanover reached out both hands toward Buffy as though she wished to help, to somehow hold Buffy up so that she would not collapse under the weight of this news.

Prediction, Buffy told herself quickly. *It isn't fact yet. We don't know it's true.*

But it felt true. The words of The Prophet were heavy with finality. With doom.

Buffy swallowed, then looked at the oily silhouette again. "Show me."

"I must only touch you, and you may see."

"Do it," Buffy instructed her.

The Prophet's slick, shimmering form slithered forward. The tear in the fabric of the world extended toward her; fingers like tendrils reached for her.

"Buffy," Willow said cautiously, a tiny bit of fear tinging her voice. "Maybe this isn't such a good—"

The Prophet touched her.

Invaded her.

Buffy screamed.

Torn away.

Buffy hurtled forward, not propelled from behind but tugged, dragged, hauled, painfully and suddenly into a black and red abyss. It felt as though only her face had been torn away, pulled on farther and farther into the chasm of infinite black before her, but the rest of her left behind, all the weight that flesh and blood and bone added to the image she had of herself. What was she? Mind and heart and soul. Face. Eyes and ears and mouth. Words.

Red whirlpools punctured the endless velvet shadow around her, flashing past as she was dragged by. As if the universe itself were wounded and bleeding.

Vaguely, in the fog that seemed to comprise her mind, a dark certainty overwhelmed her.

This was not a vision. Somehow, her spirit had been torn from her body and was now on a journey. Traveling. Hurtling out of control toward some unfathomable point in the distance.

Buffy felt her mind slipping away from her, felt herself shutting down as she was drawn through the void . . . and drawn . . . and drawn. Lulled into a kind of hibernation, aware and yet unresponsive to her surroundings.

Then, suddenly, some sense that the void was not endless, the abyss not infinite. Somewhere ahead was a barrier, a wall, and she was hurtling toward it, bound for collision. She peered into the darkness ahead but all had become black now, as though she were blind. But blind or not, she could feel it, sense its proximity as she was whipped along a course toward inevitable impact.

Collision.

Cold water splashed her face.

Shocked, Buffy stared at her fingers, splayed before her. At the grimy, cracked porcelain of the sink and the water running from the faucet. Instinctively she looked up for a mirror over the sink but there wasn't one.

Of course there isn't one. They took it away the first day, she thought. She flashed back to that time, five years before, when Clownface and Bulldog had thrown her, beaten, bloody and barely conscious, into this cell for the first time. *They didn't want you to cut your wrists.*

Like a cornered animal Buffy spun and her eyes darted around the room. The cell. Bars on the two high windows barely allowed the tiniest bit of light from the outside. Ten-foot stone walls all around. A steel door with rivets driven through it and neither handle nor knob nor even keyhole on this side.

Built for me. This was built for me.

Her hands went to the sides of her head and she squeezed her eyes closed. Then she opened them wide and gazed around the room, hugging herself tightly. Buffy knew things. She did not know how, but she *knew*.

Impossible.

But inescapably true.

She had been here, in this cell, for a very long time. Reluctantly, afraid of what she would find, she looked at her hands again. Rough, hard hands, with lines that had never been there before. She stretched, felt her body, *looked* at herself.

No thinner than before. But harder. Tighter. Rippled with muscles she remembered seeing in magazines and on television whenever they showed women who were Olympians, whose very life was exercise, exertion, sport.

But there was nothing sporting about this.

Buffy's body was taut and dangerous. She felt it, even in the way she moved. She felt like a weapon.

Gathering dust.

This cell. Endless days and nights alone, with only these four walls and the ruthless way she forged her body into this steel thing. Vampires with tattooed faces and orange flames in their eyes; they fed her, kept her alive, but nothing more. No talking, not even threats or taunts. Only the toning of her body kept her sane, that focus on the day she would escape.

And in time, even that focus blurred and there was only the routine of exercise. Hope dimmed.

These aren't my memories. Can't be my memories. I remember yesterday. They took Giles. Camazotz is preying on Sunnydale. Lucy Hanover came in my dreams and Willow summoned her and . . .

Buffy stared down at her hands again. And they *were* her hands. Just as the memories of this room— month after month becoming intimate with these four walls, eating the awful slop they fed her, and waiting for an opening—just as those recollections were hers.

Lines on her hands.

Five years since she had been put into this room.

"No," she whispered. *It's impossible.*

"No!" she screamed.

With a roar of fury and hatred surging up from her chest, Buffy ran full tilt at the door. Though her body still felt foreign to her, she loved the way it moved. Fluid and powerful and deadly. She launched a drop kick at the steel door, slammed into it hard enough to rattle her jaw, then fell to the ground and banged her head hard on the stone floor. Adrenaline screamed in her, and she pushed the pain away. With a flip, she was up on her feet, and she kicked and punched at the door with only the echo of her own grunts in the room to accompany her.

Several minutes passed. She slowed, breathing heavily.

The adrenaline subsided. The ache in her skull and the pain in her bloody, ravaged knuckles was real. The skin on her fists was scraped raw. Buffy reached up to touch the back of her head, where she'd struck the floor, and her fingers came back streaked with blood.

She would heal quickly. After all, she was the Slayer. But the wounds were real. This was real.

Even as her mind recoiled in horror at these thoughts, even as she examined her body and her surroundings, she felt her memory of the battle with Camazotz begin to dim. Desperate to save Giles, they had summoned Lucy Hanover. Lucy had called upon an entity known only as The Prophet, who promised Buffy a vision of the future, a vision that might help her prevent it and save Giles's life.

The Prophet had touched her.

But this was no vision.

Whatever The Prophet had done, somehow she was not nineteen anymore. Buffy Summers was twenty-four, at least. Maybe twenty-five. Somehow, the entity had torn her spirit from her body that day, years ago, and thrust it into the future, into this body.

Her memories of that day faded, now. Though she knew in her heart that in some way it had happened only moments before, she remembered it as though years had passed. But there was a blank spot there as well . . . a period of days she did not remember at all . . . the time during which she had been captured. A gap in her memory existed between The Prophet touching her and the day when Clownface and Bull-dog threw her into her cell.

For more than five years, she had wondered what had happened in that dead space in her memory, that blackout.

No. It isn't me. I haven't been here. It never happened, she reminded herself. And yet there was no longer any doubt that this was real. She could feel every muscle, every scratch, every sensation. This was her own body, her own life, and yet somehow her nineteen-year-old mind had been fast-forwarded into an older body, a dark, horrible future.

And all she could do was pace the cell. Work her body. Train for the day the vampires let their guard down.

Days passed. She trained and slept and washed and trained. They brought food before dawn and after dusk, always armed, always in groups of three or more. Made her stand in the far corner, afraid to have her come too close, as though she were a wild animal.

It made her smile.

* * *

Perhaps two weeks later, they brought the girl.

It was dark when they threw her into the cell, bruised and bloody but conscious. Alive. The girl was a brunette, dark and exotic. Italian, maybe, Buffy thought. Tall, but young. Even through the blood, when she looked up with her defiant, crazy eyes, Buffy could see that she was just a kid. Not more than sixteen, maybe less.

For a moment Buffy only stood there staring at her, five years without human contact having built up a callus on her heart and soul. She was two people in one, two Buffys at one time, the hardened prisoner and the young warrior. Then suddenly it was as though the part of her mind that was still nineteen simply woke up. It was as though she had been frozen in this body from the moment she had realized what had happened to her.

Now she thawed.

Ice melted away from her true self.

Buffy went to the girl, reached down for her. "Are you all right?"

The girl's eyes changed then. She blinked and her mouth opened with an expression of absolute astonishment.

"Oh my God," the girl whispered, voice cracking. "You're . . . you're her, aren't you?"

"I'm not tracking."

The girl backed away, stood up slowly, painfully, and stared at her. "You're Buffy Summers. I've seen pictures."

"Yeah? How do I look?"

Beaten, bleeding, the girl actually laughed. A discordant sound, but a welcome one just the same. "Like hell," she said. "You look like hell."

"Who are you?" Buffy asked.

But she thought she already knew the answer.

"I'm August."

Buffy frowned. "You're a month?"

"It's my name," the girl said, annoyed. She wiped blood from under her nose but it was still bleeding. "I'm the Slayer now."

Buffy closed her eyes. Shook her head to clear her mind. She felt a little unsteady on her feet. So many questions. But if this girl was a Slayer, what did that mean for—

"Faith?"

August nodded. "Six months ago. They tried for years to catch her, the way they . . . the way they did you. If it weren't for her they'd have the whole West Coast by now, maybe more. At least that's what my Watcher says. They caught her outside of L.A., I heard."

Wary, maybe even a little afraid, the girl gave Buffy a cautious look. "Have you been here all along? All this time?"

No. I just got here. A couple of weeks ago. I'm not supposed to be here. Those were the first thoughts in her head, but even as they flickered through her mind she knew they weren't really true.

"All this time," Buffy told her. She turned her back

on the girl and began to pace the room. "And now I've got company."

"But haven't you tried to—"

Buffy spun to face her, nearly growling. "Every day. What the hell do you think I am? I'm the Slayer."

"You're *a* Slayer," August corrected. "Not even the main one anymore. Not for a long time. The Council, they just call you the Lost Slayer now. Not even your name."

Buffy took that in. In her mind she reached back to the moment she knew was truly hers, where her mind belonged. Her soul . . . where her soul had been pushed away, into the here and now, and her body left behind. Hijacked.

What had happened between then and now? Where were they all? What had happened to Giles?

"How much territory do they control? Camazotz and the vampires?" she asked.

August seemed deeply troubled. She stared at the steel door, then turned back to look at Buffy, sizing her up.

"Well?" Buffy prodded.

"Sunnydale. A few other towns. Maybe a thirty mile radius around."

"And nobody knows?"

"Nobody believes," August told her. "Nobody wants to believe. That's how they win. Spin control. Marketing the illusion that everything's normal. Plenty of humans willing to help for a piece of the power."

"God," Buffy rasped.

"So there's no way out of here?" August asked, her voice taking on a kind of quiet desperation, as if she had surrendered a part of herself. "You've tried everything?"

"Five years is a long time," Buffy told her. "Maybe with two of us now it'd be different, but I figure they'll just send more guards now to bring the meals."

"Then I guess we don't have any choice," August said softly. Her eyes filled with moisture and she wiped at them bitterly. Then she took a breath and steadied herself, a grim expression on her face.

"Again, not tracking," Buffy told her.

August stared at her as though she were stupid. "They captured you because they finally got smart. If you don't kill the Slayer, there won't be another one. Keep you in here . . ." She whirled around, threw her arms up in near hysteria. "Keep us in here, and there'll never be another Slayer."

Buffy stared at her. "You have a gift for stating the obvious."

"You're just going to let them? There's nothing to stop them from spreading even further now." August bit her lip, shook her head and hugged herself as though attempting to deny the thoughts that were filling her head.

"It sucks. It truly does," Buffy said, hearing the pain in her own voice. The despair. "But until they get stupid, or let down their guard, there's nothing we can do."

August pushed a lock of her short, black hair behind her ears. She would not turn her iron-gray eyes up to look at Buffy.

"There's something I can do," she said softly.

One eyebrow raised, Buffy studied her. "What's that? What can you do?"

Finally, August met her gaze. Her soft eyes had hardened again. Crazy, defiant eyes. Eyes cold and decisive.

"I can kill you."

To Be Continued . . .

ABOUT THE AUTHOR

CHRISTOPHER GOLDEN is the award-winning, *L.A. Times* best-selling author of such novels as *Straight on 'Til Morning, Strangewood, Prowlers,* and the *Body of Evidence* series of teen thrillers.

Golden has also written a great many books and comic books related to the TV series *Buffy the Vampire Slayer* and *Angel.* His other comic book work includes stories featuring such characters as Batman, Wolverine, Spider-Man, The Crow, and Hellboy, among many others.

As a pop culture journalist, he was the editor of the Bram Stoker Award–winning book of criticism, *CUT!: Horror Writers on Horror Film,* and co-author of both *Buffy the Vampire Slayer: The Monster Book* and *The Stephen King Universe.*

Golden was born and raised in Massachusetts, where he still lives with his family. He graduated from

Tufts University. He is currently at work on the third book in the *Prowlers* series, *Predator and Prey,* and a new novel for Signet called *The Ferryman.* There are more than four million copies of his books in print. Please visit him at www.christophergolden.com.

They're real,
and they're here...

When Jack Dwyer's best friend
Artie is murdered, he is devastated.
But his world is turned upside down
when Artie emerges from the ghostlands
to bring him a warning.

With his dead friend's guidance,
Jack learns of the Prowlers. They
move from city to city, preying on
humans until they are close to being
exposed, then they move on.

Jack wants revenge. But even as he
hunts the Prowlers, he marks himself—
and all of his loved ones—as prey.

Don't miss the exciting
new series from

BESTSELLING AUTHOR
CHRISTOPHER GOLDEN!

PROWLERS

POCKET
PULSE

PUBLISHED BY POCKET BOOKS